UNDER A
SHOOTING
STAR

UNDER A
SHOOTING
STAR

MAXINE TROTTIER

Stoddart Kids
TORONTO · NEW YORK

Published in Canada in 2001 by Stoddart Kids, a division of
Stoddart Publishing Co. Limited
895 Don Mills Road, 400-2 Park Centre, Toronto, Ontario M3C 1W3

Published in the United States in 2002 by Stoddart Kids, a division of
Stoddart Publishing Co. Limited
PMB 128, 4500 Witmer Estates, Niagara Falls, New York 14305-1386

www.stoddartkids.com

To order Stoddart books please contact General Distribution Services
In Canada tel. (416) 213-1919   Fax (416) 213-1917
Email cservice@genpub.com
In the United States Toll-free tel. 1-800-805-1083   Toll-free fax 1-800-481-6207
Email gdsinc@genpub.com

05   04   03   02   01   1   2   3   4   5

Canadian Cataloguing in Publication Data
Trottier, Maxine
Under a shooting star

(The circle of silver chronicles)
ISBN 0-7737-6228-0

1. Canada — History — War of 1812 — Fiction.   I. Title.
II. Series: Trottier, Maxine. Circle of silver chronicles.

PS8589.R685U52   2001   C813'.54   C2001-902292-1
PZ7.T7532Un   2001

Cover Illustration: Al Van Mil
Cover and Text Design: Tannice Goddard

THE CANADA COUNCIL | LE CONSEIL DES ARTS
FOR THE ARTS | DU CANADA
SINCE 1957 | DEPUIS 1957

*We acknowledge for their financial support of our publishing program the Canada Council,
the Ontario Arts Council, and the Government of Canada through the
Book Publishing Industry Development Program (BPIDP).*

Printed and bound in Canada

For Kelly and Kristin

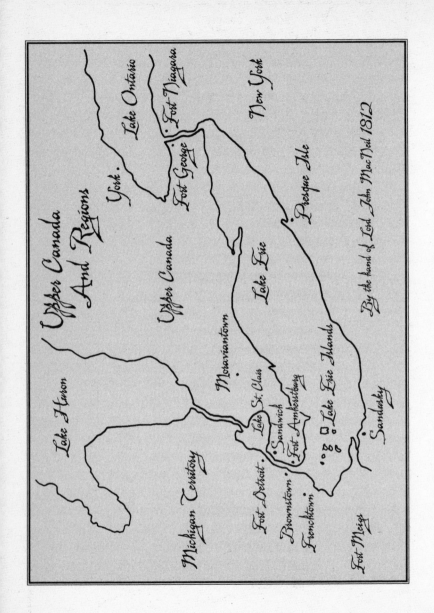

Upper Canada
And Regions

Lake Huron

Lake Ontario

York.

Fort Niagara

New York

Upper Canada

Fort George

Presque Isle

Lake Erie

Moraviantown

Michigan Territory

Lake St. Clair

Sandwich

Fort Amherstburg

Lake Erie Islands

Fort Detroit.

Brownstown.

Frenchtown.

Sandusky

Fort Meigs

By the hand of Lord John MacNeil 1812

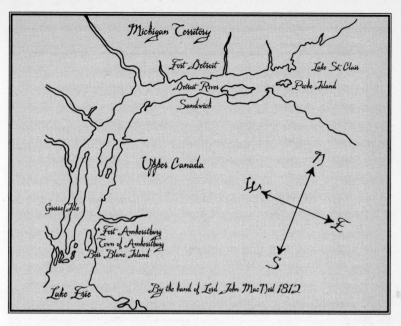

Michigan Territory

Fort Detroit

Lake St. Clair

Detroit River

Peche Island

Sandwich

Upper Canada

N

W

E

Grosse Isle

S

Fort Amherstburg
Town of Amherstburg
Bois Blanc Island

Lake Erie

By the hand of Lord John MacNeil 1812

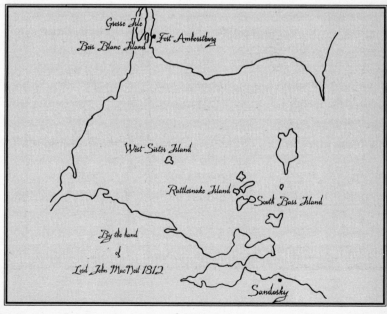

Grosse Isle

Bois Blanc Island

Fort Amherstburg

West Sister Island

Rattlesnake Island

South Bass Island

By the hand

of

Lord John MacNeil 1812

Sandusky

The Doigs

Wallace
m.
Sali of the Miami

Sean   Alex   Hamish
m.
Niki of
the Oneida

Owela
m.
Charlotte
MacNeil

Thomas

Sarah
m.
Jamie

Edward

The MacNeils

Captain the Lord James
m.
Lady Emma Pitt

David   John   Jane
m.
Henry
Fitzwalter

The Stacks

Patrick

m.   m.
Katherine   Margaret
West   Eyre

Elias

Katherine
m.
Karl Kimmerling

Kate   Anne

The LaButtes

Pierre
m.
Marie Roy

Pierre
m.
Marie Beaubien

Julian
m.
Marie Lesperance

Pierre

There are many kinds of courage. One sort ends in glory, and your name lives on, carved forever upon a towering monument. Another is of a more quiet nature. No fanfare blows; no golden medal shines as a reward. To face each day with a firm resolve, to take life's journey a single step at a time, no matter how bitter your losses or grief, may seem small and ordinary. But it is not. That sort of bravery is something that must be experienced to be understood; it can be like the hardest rite of passage. As the summer of 1812 trembled at the brink of war, Edward Wolf MacNeil did not yet understand the nature of courage. He soon would.

CHAPTER
ONE

It was a horrible storm in early July, one of the worst anyone could recall for many years. Lake Erie was not to be trusted, for a blow like this could come up out of nowhere — the sky would turn purple and huge waves would build. A ship could easily be lost. And that was the dreadful truth, for at this moment the vessel nearing South Bass Island was going down.

The old merchant schooner *Patience* would not swim for more than a few minutes longer. She had hit a reef out on the lake, and though her bottom had only brushed the limestone, she had been running with the wind at a fearsome speed. Several planks had sprung and water began to pour in. Her captain and crew had fought hard the last hour, but she was taking on more water than her pump could handle. The mainmast was gone and shreds of rigging littered the deck. Wind shrieked in what was left of the shrouds around the mizzenmast. Sailors struggled to launch the ship's boat.

"Edward! You must bring up the girls. It cannot wait a minute longer!" bellowed the captain, calling to the young man who stood frozen on the deck. "The ship will go down and take you with her!"

Edward struggled to the hatch, pulled off its canvas cover, and staggered down the companionway ladder. Below was chaos as desperate as that outside. Lockers had spilled their contents everywhere, water was knee-deep, and the steady thrum and moan of the rigging was a hopeless sound. Two girls were just picking themselves up from where they had tumbled in the ship's last drunken lurch. They were soaked to the skin and shaken.

"We are sinking!" cried the older girl. She pushed dripping strands of hair from her face. "The captain said to stay below, but we will die here!"

"You will not die. Kate, Anne, you must come on deck now," Edward said as calmly as he could. It was a struggle to remain standing upright at the foot of the companionway. "They are launching the small boat and you will get into it. I am certain we are not far from one of the islands. All will be well." The ship gave a long, low groan and heeled deeply as a powerful blast of wind hit her.

"But what of you? You must come with us," the younger girl, Anne, begged him, squinting through water-spotted spectacles. She pushed them more securely onto her nose and tightened the cord that would keep them around her neck if they fell.

"Surely you will come with us!" Kate cried. She looked down in panic as she felt the water rising.

"I will be just behind you. We will stay together. Now, Anne, go carefully. Kate, hold onto her hand and you must hold onto mine. The wind is fearful."

They climbed the ladder, gasping as water poured down upon them. On deck they could barely stand. Kate stumbled and slid across the planks toward the dark water, pulling Anne with her, but Edward held hard onto Kate's hand, and unceremoniously pulled them both to their feet. The launch was already in the water. It bobbed up and down wildly with each enormous wave that swept by. The six sailors in it struggled to keep the boat from pulling away while two seamen helped the girls down and then climbed in themselves.

"What of you, sir?" Edward shouted back to the captain, but the man would not leave his vessel until all were safe. Edward fell to his knees as lakewater poured over the side. Rain and spray slashed at his face. Then the ship slipped down a steep wave, steerage gone, and veered wildly. She turned on her side, and the yard on her mizzen dipped into the churning lake and broke away as the sail filled with foaming water. A wave flooded into the launch. Clinging to a line, Edward heard terrified screams as the small boat tipped and then it righted itself. Lightning arced across the sky, thunder answered, and only Anne was inside the launch now. The sailors and Kate were nearby, struggling to stay above the waves.

With a deep, wrenching groan, *Patience* began to sink in earnest. His eyes on Kate, Edward dived into the lake; the captain jumped into the churning water moments later. In the chilling rain, the water felt strangely warm. Edward's clothing pulled him down; his shoes were like heavy weights. He kicked them off and swam upward. When his head broke the surface, he gasped a great breath of air mixed with spray. The ship and the men in the water were gone. Kate clung to the side of the launch; Anne unable to pull her in.

Edward swam hard, choking when spray lashed across the water. He reached the launch and with all his strength grasped Kate by the hips and shoved her up and over the rail. She tumbled into the boat in a tangle of soaked skirts just as a huge wave began to rise under the launch.

"Edward!" she cried. "My hand! Take my hand!" Kate leaned out as far as she dared. Edward's fingers brushed hers, their hands clasped for a heartbeat and then the force of the wave pulled them apart. Edward slid down one side of the wave as the launch disappeared behind it in the heavy rain.

Edward was alone on the lake.

◇ ◇

The water was quiet. The fierce storm had passed and the afternoon sun shone on a sandy beach. Stretched on his belly, Edward Wolf MacNeil woke, but did not immediately open his eyes. A gull screeched above him. He struggled to sit up and felt bile rising in his throat. On his hands and knees, he vomited helplessly — dry heaves mostly, since there was not much in his belly at all.

Edward wiped his mouth on his sleeve and sat in the sand. His shoes were gone. The back of his clothing, a cotton shirt and canvas trousers, was dry, but the front was damp. He was battered, scraped raw, and horribly thirsty. Realizing his head ached dreadfully, he touched it. His fingers came away red and sticky with blood that was matted into his scalp. It came back to him then — the storm, the captain jumping from the ship. He had swum blindly, hopelessly, not knowing how far he was from the islands that were out here. He had thought himself unable to swim another minute when a wave washed over him and drove him down. His bare feet had brushed rippled sand. The next wave had sent him up on a beach in a rush of foam and seaweed. He had struggled to crawl above the grasping fingers of the waves and collapsed, exhausted upon the sand. Shock turned his stomach yet again and Edward felt bile rise in his throat as he remembered the girls. Had they lived? He must find them.

Edward carefully climbed to his feet. He was a sailor, a strong young man of fifteen years. Long dark hair, normally worn in a plait like the other fellows of his crew, had come undone and draped down his back. He had his father's clear gray eyes and his mother's high cheekbones — an oddly exotic combination that puzzled most people until he spoke. For although Edward was of mixed blood, English and Oneida, he was the son of a gentleman, James MacNeil, and the nephew of Lord John MacNeil, the King's own artist in Canada. He had been journeying as a passenger on *Patience* to his uncle's home on Pêche Island in the Detroit River when the storm struck.

Edward peered out across the water, squinting into the haze. To the south and east was one island; to the northwest was another. He was certain the spot on which he now stood was South Bass Island. The mainlands of both Canada and the United States lay to the north and, although he could not see it, he knew the river was less than a day's sail away.

Edward had been at sea since he was eleven years old. The Royal Navy was out of the question, his parents and his Uncle John had said: better to serve upon one of the MacNeil's merchant vessels.

"It is the most natural thing for you to go to sea, Edward. All the MacNeils are sailors, as you well know. There is the *Marie Roy* for the first while," Lord MacNeil had written from Canada. "She will be a fine ship upon which to learn your seamanship, and you will be safe from the call of war there. You will be an ordinary seaman at first so that you may learn your craft from the bottom up. I will sail with you for the first year or so, just to see how you fare, although I am certain the life will suit you. Some day, God willing, you will have a ship of your own."

The life had, indeed, suited him from the beginning. He worked as hard as any of the other ship's boys, learning every task that had to be done upon a vessel. It was not just a matter of handling sails— there was navigation and keeping the ship clean, scouring the decks with stones each morning.

In the year they had spent together, Edward had come to love his uncle greatly. The two of them were much alike, although fifty years separated them. Often when Edward's watch was finished, they would sit together at the ship's rail. His uncle would draw the sailors or the ship itself. The day that Lord MacNeil left the ship to return to his island was a sad one for Edward.

Regarding one thing, however, Lord MacNeil had not been entirely correct. Relations between England and the United States had grown worse and worse. British warships stopped American vessels and pressed their men into service. Not even British merchant vessels were safe. In spite of Lord MacNeil's connections at Court, it was possible that the same thing might happen to the crew of the *Marie Roy*. At Halifax, a letter had been waiting for Edward this past fall. He was to voyage inland to sail on the MacNeil merchant ship *Odonata* on Lake Ontario for a summer. Then he would come to the island to stay with his uncle until things settled out.

Edward obeyed all orders without question, but within himself, he had bridled against leaving the ship he now felt was his home. He was no untried boy and had been at sea all this while. He could load and fire both a musket and a swivel gun. A cannon was not a mystery to him either, and he felt no fear at the thought of standing with his shipmates to defend the ship. How odd it would be to sail what seemed to be rather small lakes after the vast reaches of the Atlantic.

In the end, nothing his parents or his uncle had ever told him had prepared him for it all. The lakes and the country had surprised him greatly. Lake Ontario had been a cold, forbidding ocean of fresh water. The Niagara River had been impossible, its current frightful and the falls shocking in their power. And Lake Erie? Lake Erie had just torn a ship apart and perhaps even killed all of its crew. None of the sailors on *Patience* had been able to swim, he knew. Few sailors could. And the girls! He swallowed painfully at the thought of the Kimmerling sisters.

Edward began to walk down the beach, his knees shaky. Everything I had is gone, he thought. He reached inside his shirt and pulled out a pendant of ivory carved in the shape of a wolf's head. He rubbed it between his fingers and carefully tucked it back inside. At least that was still there. Then he heard the sound of high voices. Anne, with Kate behind her, came tearing around the stand of trees just ahead.

"Edward! There you are. And you are alive!" shouted Anne. The light glinted off the glass of her spectacles. Tied around her neck, the precious spectacles — a gift from a wealthy cousin — had stayed on in spite of the storm. Anne was a carefree child of twelve years and Edward loved her smile. What a relief it was to see her whole. She stopped, waved her arms above her head, and began to run once more.

Edward ran as well. He felt strong at first, but then he felt all the blood leave his head. Pinpricks of light flashed in his eyes, the world roared around him, his knees gave way, and he crumpled to the sand.

◇ ◇

When he woke, it was well past dawn the next day. His head was resting in Kate's lap, as was Anne's. Carefully, very carefully, he sat up. They were still on the beach close to the water. Anne's eyes opened instantly and she sat up as well. They both watched him cautiously; Kate put the back of her hand to Edward's cheek and then onto his forehead. A year ago, unaccustomed to such forwardness in a female, Edward would have flinched away as far as he could without falling backward into the sand. Now he did not think it forward at all, so fond of her had he become. "I am fine, Kate. How long have I been unconscious? When did the ship sink?"

"It sank the night before last," she explained. "You are not fine. It was the blow to your head, Edward. You moved too quickly. Surely sleep has helped."

"Does it hurt, Edward?" asked Anne.

"Not so much," answered Edward, grimacing at the throbbing that was slowly beginning to fade. "You did not sit up all night, did you, Kate?"

"Of course not." He could see the lie in her tired face. "I so feared for you," Kate whispered. "We washed ashore in the darkness during the storm. We could not keep the waves from pulling the launch back out. Then we could not find you or anyone else." She swallowed several times, blinked hard, and then looked at him in her direct manner. "When the launch tipped I thought none of us would live."

"We did," Edward said quietly. Although I am not certain of the others, he thought. "You need not fuss over me, Kate."

Kate shook her head in exasperation. "Edward MacNeil, you know quite well I am not fussing. I simply wish to assure myself that you have no fever."

"You know that Kate often helps our mother with her

midwifery," Anne offered. Shaken, but now reassured with Edward awake, she tried a smile at him and flipped her honey-colored hair over her shoulders. It now had a rat nest–like arrangement. She stood and walked to the lake. Holding the skirts of her plain gown of faded blue cotton well above her ankles, Anne rinsed the sand from her legs.

"A midwife," Edward said faintly. "I hardly require a midwife."

"No, but you need someone to look after your wounds. I will do so. I feel it is my responsibility," Kate announced, desperate for anything normal. "I looked after my uncle all last winter. He was an impossible patient. Surely I can do the same for you."

Edward looked carefully at Kate. Was she injured? Her pale gold hair hung in strings. There were violet shadows under her eyes. They were interesting eyes, blue and tilted up just a bit. A scrape ran along one side of her face. Her pink gingham day dress, simple and high-waisted, hung damply from her shoulders. "I am your friend, Kate. We are all battered and we must look after each other. I promised your Uncle Elias when we were still at Fort George that I would see you safely to your parents' home at Sandusky." He laughed, but there was no sound of humor in it. "It appears I must do so for a longer while than we thought. I do wish the circumstances were different."

"What of the others, Edward?" asked Kate. "Might any of them have lived or are we alone?" Her voice caught. "I am certain I saw a body floating out in the water yesterday." Anne stood very still by the lake's edge; behind the spectacles, her hazel eyes were huge. The reality of the storm rushed over them all. Edward could hear only the soft lapping of the waves and the patter of poplar leaves in the soft breeze as they stared silently at each other.

"There are other islands here, and they may have reached one or another. But none of them could swim, Kate. I fear they are all gone. God help them." How close they had all come to the same fate. There was a wash of deep violet cloud low on the horizon to the west. Distant thunder gave an ominous rumble. Edward shook himself; in this heat he knew another summer storm could easily be brewing after the one of the night before. "Hurry. I do not like the nature of the sky."

He slowly stood and looked up and down the beach. Things had washed up above the high water mark. There were a few torn hammocks, several planks, and the shattered end of a yard. A sea chest floated in the calm water a dozen yards away. Edward waded in, ducked his head, and swam to it. The water stung his wounds and his muscles burned with the effort of pulling it ashore.

The storm passed to the north. Its purple clouds danced with lightning and long shrouds of rain streamed out behind, but the island was spared. During that day they slowly made a rough camp in the shelter of a stand of maples where bushes would give some protection. Anne and Kate carried up the small chest and lifted its lid. It had been unlocked, and the poor clothing inside it was damp. There was a striker, flints, bits of charcloth, and some tow for tinder in a sealed tin. A chipped mug and two wooden bowls with a single spoon were wrapped in a cloth.

I have lost everything I owned, but this man lost his life, thought Edward, and he felt a great rush of shame for even thinking that belongings might be more important than that. He spread the hammocks out on low bushes; it would not take them long to dry. He worked hard, but he truly had no reserves of strength to call upon. By the time he had gathered whatever sticks of driftwood he could see, with which to make a fire, Edward's face was pale beneath his tan. His belly and ribs still ached from the vomiting, and the throbbing in his head was sickening.

In the evening, a fierce sun sank into the lake. Edward's belly growled, but there was no food. Dead fish littered the beach and a few floated belly-up in the water. Anne splashed out to gather them, for they might be fresh enough to eat after all. Kate and Edward watched her pick them up and examine each carefully before setting them in the bowl. Edward made a small fire. The knife he wore in a sheathe at the back of his belt was sharp. He cleaned several fish, sniffed at them, and pronounced, "They are not spoiled." He looked questioningly at Kate, who nodded in clear distaste.

"We must eat something," she admitted.

Later, when Anne was asleep beneath the shelter of a hammock, Edward and Kate sat together by the fire. Since meeting them a year ago, he had become very fond of both of the girls. They had met quite by accident in the town of Newark near Fort George, when Edward's ship stopped there. How strange that his Uncle John and their uncle, Elias Stack, had been fast friends since before the Revolutionary War. It did not take so very long for the same sort of friendship to begin to grow among Edward, Kate, and Anne.

He had no sisters, and the females at home in England, whom he saw now and again at dinners or while riding, were delicate and ladylike. Kate Kimmerling was a different sort. The same age as Edward, she was tall and boyishly slim with fine, pale skin. Bookish and self-taught, for her family was too poor to have considered a formal education for either of the daughters, she faced life with confidence. She was a wonderful companion, for she did not practice any sort of feminine wiles upon him. Although she did not know it, he considered her to be the sister he had never had.

"Let me plait your hair for you, and you shall do mine," said Kate. "Tie mates. That is what we shall be."

"I have no comb," Edward protested.

"I have one, though how it stayed in my pocket I have no idea," said Kate. "I know very well that you do not have lice, so I hardly mind sharing with you." Edward winced when the comb nicked the cut on his scalp. Clucking her tongue, Kate dipped a rag in water, dabbed at the cut, and heaved a sigh. "I can do nothing else. You are fortunate that it did not need stitching. My needles and threads and everything else I had went down with the ship." Her voice trailed off and Edward thought she might be close to weeping, a thing she truly loathed, but her fingers started braiding.

"What will happen to us, Edward?" she asked quietly. She tied the end of his braid with a bit of thread that she pulled from a tear in her dress.

"Tomorrow we will look for the farm that is here just inside the bay. My uncle sent a map of this island once in one of his letters. The man who owns it is an American. Surely he will have a boat of some sort. We shall convince him to take you home and me to the island. It is a sail of only perhaps fifteen miles southeast to Sandusky and nearly the same distance north from here to the Detroit River. It is that, or he will spend the summer with you, me, and Anne until we can get word to our families."

"Anne!" Edward could hear the sound of the smile in her words. "The prospect of a summer with her would be certain to convince the fellow to take us anywhere." Anne groaned contentedly in her sleep. "She acts as though we were not nearly killed," Kate whispered faintly. "I could not get out of the water fast enough, and yet there she was today, still completely at home in it."

"I could teach you to swim," Edward suggested. "If you wish, that is."

"I certainly do not," huffed Kate, and Edward felt mild shock at her tone. Seeing his distress, for she could be quite sharp, she said more kindly, "I dislike the water even more than I did before." Her voice fell off and she buried her head against her knees for a moment. "You and I are very different."

Edward stiffened. "I beg your pardon. I am quite aware that we are different," he said in a silky tone. This was the first time anything the least unpleasant had come up between them.

"No, no," Kate protested. "I did not mean anything except that you have a great fondness for swimming and I detest it."

He watched her to see if she was speaking honestly. Perhaps she was. In a way, Edward no longer cared. At home in England as a small child, he had not really been aware of how different his family and he, in particular, were. The MacNeils' eccentricity was excused only by the fact that they were peers greatly favored at Court. "That is what you meant, is it?" Edward asked. He looked down at his hands with their tanned skin — skin that was such a contrast to hers.

"What else might I have meant?"

"I am of mixed blood, Kate, as you well know," Edward said stiffly. "It was of no significance at home that my father is English and my mother Native. Even aboard our ship crossing the ocean it had little meaning. Once I came to the lakes, I had rather a different experience."

"You have told me of this before, Edward. You are behaving in a ridiculous manner!" she snapped. "This is North America. We are almost all an odd mixture here. You might be part goose and it would mean less than nothing to me. Now my hair," said Kate, turning her back on him. Edward took the comb from her and began to pull it through her thick locks. "I meant nothing at all, Edward. Truly."

"I beg your pardon for thinking otherwise, but I have seen the looks and heard the name often enough to be thoroughly sick of them. Half-breed." His hands pulled at her hair roughly, bitterness overcoming him for a moment, but she said nothing, only gasped a little. "There, now I have hurt you, Kate. Forgive me. I will go more carefully." He finished in silence and gave her back the comb.

"Edward, you are the closest friend I have ever had. I do not make friends easily," she confessed with some discomfort. "I have never before felt I needed a friend. There was always Anne, Mama, and Father, and they were enough. Uncle Elias also, of course. How grateful I am that we were able to spend last winter with him when he was ill. Besides, the fact that we were there brought us together. I value you as a friend, Edward, and not simply for all you have done." Her solemn expression disappeared as an idea came to her. "Let us make a promise that we shall always be friends. We will surely part in time, but let us swear that nothing will change our friendship."

Edward nearly smiled, for with those words, she seemed suddenly very young to him, but he saw how important this was to her. "Very well. Let us swear on this." He picked up the wolf's head on its thong. "On this I vow my friendship to you, Kate. Nothing will ever change it."

"And I promise that I will always hold your friendship dearly. Nothing in life will ever change it. Now let us sleep if we can. Will it be a long walk to the farm?" She settled herself under the hammock, next to Anne.

"Only a few miles," Edward told her. He stretched out on the ground, his hands behind his head, and stared at the stars that were beginning to come out. "This has been horrible for you, but it will soon be over."

In the morning though, when they walked from the trees into the clearing where the farm lay, Edward saw that he had been wrong. The farm was a black, burned ruin, silent and empty. There would be no escape from the island any time soon.

CHAPTER
TWO

"What has happened here?" wondered Kate. Always composed, just a hint of fear now edged her words. "Where are the people?"

They walked slowly past the ruins of the house and barn. Here was a small shed that had also burned to the ground. The stinking bodies of pigs and cows lay bloated in the grass. Pots, dishes filled with rainwater, and a bashed-in chest of sodden clothing were scattered nearby. A rag doll with the head ripped off spilled out its wet stuffing. This is no accident or act of nature, thought Edward, and a great discomfort filled him. He bent down and picked up a tin cup. Fingering the hole in it, he said uneasily, "This was made by a musket ball."

"Why would there be fighting here?" asked Kate. "Anne, do not wander!" Kate's tone was sharp, and for once Anne obeyed without question.

"I have no idea," Edward answered. "Uncle John has always said that this end of the lake is a quiet place and well settled. There has been no fighting here since the French and Indian War. The last of that was in 1760."

Edward lifted his shoulders. "I do not like the way this feels. Let us get away from here." They hurried back into the shelter of the woods. Edward took a deep breath of clean air.

"Is that a sail?" Anne asked incredulously. She pointed to a spit of land around which a vessel was just coming. The early morning's breeze was gone and the vessel, a sailing boat of no more than thirty feet, was drifting in. The heady sound of cicadas came from the trees. Edward felt a tickle of sweat not entirely caused by the heat, creep down his neck.

"It is flying an American flag!" said Kate in excitement. She began to move forward, to run to the beach and call out, but before she could, Edward grabbed her arm.

"Wait," he cautioned. "We must be certain they are not a threat to us. For all I am aware, they may have burned the farm and are coming back to pick it over."

"Your imagination is spectacular, Edward. That boat is our only means of leaving this island." She tried to pull away, but Edward's grip was firm.

"What if they are pirates, Kate?" asked Anne dramatically. She opened her eyes wide and moaned. "What if they burned the farm and captured all the people? They will take us prisoners as well."

Kate made a rude noise. "Pirates, indeed! Very well. We shall wait, but not for long."

They watched the men on the boat drop its sails as it slid toward the center of the bay. Edward heard the sound of an anchor's splash, and then the men lowered a canoe. Their voices carried over the water, and although he could not make out what they were saying, it was clear that someone would stay onboard while the others came ashore. They paddled toward the island, beached their canoe, and lifted out muskets.

"I knew they were pirates!" whispered Anne.

"Hush!" Kate hissed. Anne stuck her tongue out and smiled sweetly, for she knew Kate could do nothing in return.

Edward heard one of the men talk of rabbits and, with a sense of relief, he realized they had simply come here to hunt. He pointedly ignored Kate's smug look; she did very much enjoy being correct. Just as he released Kate's arm, just as he began to step out of the trees, they heard the first shot. There was more firing, wild whoops, and a cry of pain as one of the men fell into the water. "We are attacked!" someone screamed. "It is a war party!"

Kate pulled Anne into her arms to protect her, but Anne, startled by the firing of the muskets, wiggled free and bolted back into the woods. Edward did not hesitate; he pulled Kate along with him and followed Anne. Someone fired a musket and Edward felt the small, deadly wind as the ball passed by his ear. They flung themselves through the bushes where Anne was waiting, her expression terrified. Edward turned to see that Natives were now on the beach. There was the crack of musket fire and shrieks filled the air. The sailors paddled hard, trying to reach the boat, but the Natives had launched their own canoes that they had hidden in the scrub.

"Run!" Edward ordered. They heard the muskets fire

over and over again. Kate stood staring. The men scrambled onto their boat and the canoe, now empty, was set adrift. Mercifully, a light breeze had come up. The anchor had been raised, the sails frantically hoisted, and the boat was sailing out of the bay. In frustration, the war party shot at the empty canoe.

"We must find somewhere to hide. They are returning," Edward urged.

"Stay with me, Anne!" Kate shook her sister. "Do not run ahead!"

"Leave me be! I have had enough of your orders, Kate. I do not have to listen any more. You are not Mama or Father." She turned and ran back through the brush and forest, toward where the trees thinned. There were no bushes there, only elms and maples that cast deep shadows.

"No," groaned Kate. She did not know where to flee.

"Hurry! This way, Kate." Edward gave Kate a push. The bushes scratched their arms and faces as they forced their way through. We are leaving a trail they will easily follow if they have seen or heard us, he thought. I can only pray they have not.

On and on they ran. Edward could hear Kate's labored breathing, and he felt a stitch beginning in his side. Ahead, Anne stopped and waited for them. Here the trees were more widely spaced, and, where the sunlight touched the ground, tall grass grew in a field. Just ahead was a large dead elm, with great patches of its bark gone. Anne waved at them to follow, took a step backward, and disappeared. Edward blinked. One moment she had been there and now she was gone. Kate ran past him and dropped to her knees in the long grass. Edward followed her and leaned down. He could see the hole now, a cleft in the soil just wide enough to admit the body of a man. He felt a chill come over himself.

"Anne!" Kate called into the opening, heedless of whether any following Natives would take notice of her. "Can you hear me? Are you hurt?" She peered down into the hole.

"I can hear you. Do not shout. It echoes most dreadfully."

"Are you hurt, Anne?" Edward repeated as loudly as he dared. Oddly, he could see right down into the hole, where light was reflecting in a strange way.

"I have a lump on my head and all the skin is gone from one knee. It is bloody, but I am not really much damaged. Come down!" Anne's voice was strained and Edward could hear something else there. "Please!" she cried as she gave a small sob.

Kate's eyes widened. Her nails dug into Edward's arm. "She has lost her senses," she whispered to Edward in despair.

"We cannot come down, Anne. We must get you out. Stay calm. I will find something. Kate will stay here with you so that you are not alone," Edward assured her.

"But, Edward," came Anne's clear voice. It wobbled as she fought to keep it brave and steady. "I am not alone at all."

CHAPTER
THREE

"Climb down. Please, Edward." Her control was beginning to waver. "He is going to shoot me!" Anne wailed. A man's low voice called out. Edward could not understand what he said. It was not English, nor a language that he had ever heard, but the threat was unmistakable.

Kate shoved past Edward. There was a narrow rope ladder. It hung from a spike that had been pounded into a crevice in the limestone. She climbed down first; Edward came after her. Anne was standing wide-eyed and shaken. Edward looked all around in amazement. This was no cave. It was more like a room, a beautiful room studded with huge, natural crystals. Light cast by a candle burning in a tin lantern gleamed on their facets. Someone had laid down a narrow floor of planks on the bottom of the cave. Had Anne missed that floor, she would surely have been killed. A Native youth kneeled near Anne, a musket pointing up shakily at her head.

Something was wrong with him, Edward saw. Cords stood out from the Native's neck, the bulging muscles of his arms trembled, and, in spite of the dead chill here, sweat was running down his nearly naked body. "*Sheko:li*," said Edward in a steady voice. The young man blinked sweat from his eyes and turned the weapon on Edward. His brows lowered in confusion.

"What did you say?" whispered Kate.

"I greeted him. Hello," Edward told her, and he smiled cautiously at the young man. "It is Oneida, but I can see that he does not understand me." Edward's parents had spoken both English and Oneida to him all his life, and he spoke French, for all the young gentlemen in his family did so. Young gentleman, he thought ruefully. I am no gentleman to anyone here. "You are hurt, I think," he said slowly in French.

"Leave me," growled the young man in English. He winced. "And save your French. I speak your tongue, white man. This is my place. Leave me or I will shoot."

"You would shoot an unarmed female? A child? Surely not. We did not mean to come upon you. She fell down through the opening. The girls only wish to return in peace to their home in Ohio." Edward glanced at Kate and as calmly as he could he said, "Get Anne out of here quickly. I will follow you."

"Ohio? They are the women of Long Knives? But you are English!" the young man exclaimed, hearing Edward's accent. "You are my ally, then."

"What do you mean?" asked Edward.

He spoke abruptly. "We are at war. The Shawnee and all the other tribes have joined the British against the Long Knives." He stared hard at Kate. "We fight against her people. What a fine prize she would make."

"I beg your pardon!" cried Kate. "What insufferable foolishness."

"War?" Edward said slowly. His eyes met Kate's as the realization of it flooded over them. "War has been declared," he said in a whisper. "England and the United States are at war."

"I am afraid, Kate," whispered Anne. She began to cry a little. "I actually do not want to be a prisoner."

"See what you have done! You dare to frighten my sister and make her weep," Kate scolded the Native, and Edward suspected that this was a new experience for him.

"He is hurt, Anne, and desperate with pain, likely. Ignore him," said Edward.

"I may be hurt," said the Native warily, for Kate was now walking toward him, "but if you come near me, I think you will see that I have enough strength left to kill you."

"I am a healer," Kate explained, but the young man turned his face from her.

"She is mad," he said to Edward. "Keep her from me or I will end her madness."

"She is not mad! She *is* a healer. Pray, do not shoot her simply because she is foolish enough to want to help you. Is that what you call bravery?"

The young man swallowed hard, and his lowered eyes told Edward that a tender nerve had been touched. "Very well," he said gruffly. "See to my wound then, white woman."

Kate rushed forward and kneeled by his side. The

young man gasped as Kate touched his thigh. Blood oozed from a furrow, a wound clearly made by a musket ball.

"He was part of the war party," muttered Kate angrily. She glared at him and he returned her furious look. "I should leave you here to bleed, but I cannot do that. Your knife, Edward, please. I have nothing to soothe this wound, but I can bind it. My shift must do. It is clean."

He was not part of the war party, they learned. He came to this island now and again to be alone and to pray. Others visited as well these days, since the whites had begun their war against each other. Warriors had come and driven off the farmer who lived here, killed all his pigs, and had a great feast. He himself had been caught in the crossfire today between the men from the ship and the warriors. It was a stray ball that hit him as he watched at the edge of the woods, and he had quickly made his way here. The presence of the whites always caused trouble. His father hated them all, and he himself did as well. His name was Paukeesaa.

"I am Edward MacNeil."

Paukeesaa's eyes widened at this, but he said nothing.

"How did you know to hide here?" asked Anne. The young man's eyes blazed and a deep flush crept up his neck. "I have not ever had anyone say that he hated me," Anne went on. Her scraped knee forgotten, she pushed her spectacles more comfortably into place and watched Kate work with keen interest. "And simply because of the color of my skin. How strange it feels."

"You . . ." He looked up at the ceiling, searching for a

word, and then smiled bitterly at Edward and said, "All of you foul this place."

Edward put his face close to Paukeesaa's. "We did not ask to be in this cave. It was an accident. We shall leave directly. You foul it yourself with your thanklessness. She means only to help you, but you are scarcely worth it, I believe. To threaten them in this way is cowardly." Paukeesaa trembled with anger. That is it, thought Edward suddenly. He is a coward and he knows it all too well. Edward stood and pulled Kate to her feet although she had not finished tying the dressing. "Come, Anne, Kate, we will take our chances outside." Kate, however, freed her hand from his. Edward felt a strange rush of shame at the thought that because of his own blood, Kate might judge him by the way this young man was behaving.

But Kate was rigid with fury. She would not weep out of fear, but she had a tender heart and she had lived all her life surrounded by her family's love. A kind act was not ever met with such rudeness. She would not return it. "The wound is surely painful but it is not as bad as it seems. You must clean it well when you can."

Faint voices sounded in the distance from outside the cave. Paukeesaa struggled to his feet, leaning heavily on his musket, and limped to the rope ladder.

"He will give us up. I know he will," Kate whispered to Edward. "What shall we do?"

Edward said nothing at all, only gazed fixedly at Paukeesaa. The young Native looked back over his shoulder, shot an arrogant glance at Kate, but did not call out. Instead, he stood at the base of the ladder, listening. Moments passed. Someone laughed and the voices of several of the warriors rumbled out in a Native tongue. Then there was silence.

"They are leaving the island. It would have gone hard for you if you had been taken, given the mood of the people. Besides, I did not wish for them to know that I was here." He glanced at Kate, but he spoke to Edward. "I am not thankless. You did me a service and I have done one in return. I will let you stay only until I am certain they have launched their canoes and then you will leave."

"To go where?" Edward exclaimed, throwing up his hands in frustration. "You have a canoe as well, I would wager."

"What of it?" Paukeesaa shrugged carelessly. "I did not swim here."

Edward went on. "I ask only one last thing of you, and then we will be gone from your life forever. You have a canoe. Will you take us to Pêche Island?" Paukeesaa was shaking his head in refusal even before Edward finished speaking. "Then I will find the canoe and do it myself," Edward said angrily.

Paukeesaa made to raise his musket, his face dark with rage, but Anne said softly, "Your leg. It is bleeding again. Kate must dress it properly or you will not be paddling anywhere."

Lines of bright blood ran down Paukeesaa's leg. "I need clean, hot water and strips of cloth," Kate announced. She regarded Paukeesaa as though he had not just threatened them again.

"Surely you do not sleep here," wondered Anne. "It is so very cold."

Paukeesaa, though, did not answer, and the chill that hung there amongst all of them was colder than the air inside the cave.

CHAPTER
FOUR

They waited until Paukeesaa was certain the war canoes were long gone and then carefully made their way from the cave. Paukeesaa had a simple camp in the woods near the burned-out farmhouse. There Anne climbed a low-limbed tree to peer out at the lake and said that she could just see the canoes disappearing. Small embers smoldered in a shallow firepit. Paukeesaa carefully lowered himself down next to it and Edward added a few sticks. Slowly they caught fire.

There was nothing of value in the blackened ruins of the house, Kate discovered. She wrinkled her nose at the smell of charred wood. Walking slowly back, she found a small, lidded box in the brush. Most of its contents were strewn about and much trampled, but the lid had snapped shut on several old linen shirts. They would do very nicely for bandages.

Edward watched her as she worked. Paukeesaa had a small copper pail. Kate sent Anne for water and when it was heated, she unwrapped the wound and gently sponged his thigh. She showed no signs of embarrassment at being so near to his nakedness. Paukeesaa kept himself very still and did not utter a sound, although what she was doing must have been painful. The set of his features, though, showed a clear aversion to her touch. He does not know her, Edward thought. How can he dislike her so?

Kate sat back on her heels and said in a matter-of-fact manner, "I have no lint and it should be packed with lint. I had ointment and packets of herbs in my bag on the ship but it is all gone. I think that if you rest for the night it will do well enough." Paukeesaa grudgingly murmured his thanks and Kate inclined her head in acceptance. "Come with me, Anne," she said. "We will need more water."

When the girls were at the beach, Paukeesaa said to Edward, "I will take you to the island tomorrow because you are English, and so an ally of my people. But the females — they are the women of our enemies. I will take them only because of the kindness the healer has shown me."

It was an odd evening. Paukeesaa studiously ignored Kate and Anne, speaking only to Edward. There was parched corn and strips of venison jerky to eat. In spite of his harsh words, Paukeesaa shared his meager supplies with all of them. He had no blankets. The weather was very warm and so he had not needed any for the week he had planned to be here. Kate and Anne made a bed in the grass, for there was nothing else they could do. Her back against her sister, Anne fell asleep at once, and from her quiet breathing, Edward was certain Kate had as well.

When Paukeesaa heard soft snoring, he asked, "You said you are a MacNeil?"

"Yes. Edward MacNeil."

"Are you kin to the MacNeil who lives on Pêche, then? The one who makes the pictures?" Edward nodded and Paukeesaa went on. "I know of him. He is a good man for a white. If he is your kin, then I offer you my friendship, for we share more than just a common enemy."

"How kind of you to say so," Edward answered with elaborate sarcasm.

Paukeesaa, who was stretching out next to the fire, did not notice. "The island is his, as much as it might belong to anyone, but he has no objection to my people stopping there. Some say the spot where the apples grow is a sacred place. Some say ghosts haunt it. I myself only know it is a good place to pray." He picked up a twig and poked it into the fire. "How is it you are here on this island?"

Edward told him about the shipwreck. "I have seen many things since I have been at sea, but I never thought a storm like that could come up on Lake Erie." He was silent for a bit. Edward could almost feel Paukeesaa's desire to hear more, but he knew that it was not the Native way to ask such things.

Paukeesaa lost his careful control. "But you are not white, are you? I can see that now." He looked hard at Edward's face and slowly said, "No, you are not white. You dress as a white and speak as one, but you are something else. Are you a half-breed?"

"If you will consider for a moment," Kate abruptly spoke up, "your skin is not so different from his." Kate was not asleep after all. Pale with anger at the idea that Edward might be looked down upon by this dreadful Native, she had lifted herself up on her elbow and was glaring at Paukeesaa. "Are *you* a half-breed?"

Edward felt the familiar anger begin to rise within him. How he loathed the word, a word he had not ever heard in England, but they needed the help of this Paukeesaa, no matter how thoughtless he might be.

"Hush now, Kate." With cool detachment he said, "My father is an Englishman, Paukeesaa, Lord MacNeil's brother, and I am Lord MacNeil's nephew. My parents met in this country when my father was a boy. My mother is Oneida, one of the Iroquois Six Nations. They married and I was born here in my uncle's home. That makes me Canadian, I suppose. We went back to England, back to my uncle's house there, since my Aunt Jane so wished to see my father. It was a visit that turned into a rather long stay." He thought of home and it pierced him to the core. He missed his parents greatly, and he missed the old house, Brierly, with its rambling apple orchard where he had played as a child. How little he had known of the world then and how it would treat him, so sheltered had he been.

"My mother was born into the wolf clan and that makes it my clan as well," Edward went on, "although I have never really had a sense of belonging to it." He pulled out his ivory pendant and Paukeesaa leaned forward. "My uncle gave me this when I was aboard the

Marie Roy. It came from a large woolly creature that they say once lived in the far north."

"Who made this?" Paukeesaa took the wolf's head from Edward's fingers. He turned it over in his hand and then held it up by its thong. In spite of his reserve, he smiled delightedly to see the perfect little creature.

"I did. I have some skill in working with my hands. It does seem to run through the family. It is a sort of carving that sailors call scrimshaw." It had taken him many hours to carve the small image, to add the fine details and the fierce, glowering eyes.

Paukeesaa dropped the pendant and glanced over at Kate. "Do the females belong to you?" he asked in French.

"Do not do that!" Kate sputtered. "I cannot speak French! It is exceedingly bad-mannered."

"No," Edward answered in English. He felt a powerful desire to laugh, not at Paukeesaa's words, but at the idea of either of the Kimmerling girls belonging to anyone. He went on in an intense voice. "They are my friends — my very dear friends. We met at Fort George. Our ship stopped there now and again, you see. They were in the town of Newark nearby.

"When we left, I swore to their uncle, Elias Stack, that I would take care of them until they reached their home near Sandusky. Elias is an old friend of my uncle and father." The image of Elias flashed into Edward's mind. He was an old man of some eighty-four years, white-haired, but as strong and as hale as a gnarled oak that has withstood many storms. Pneumonia had caused him to suffer most grievously two springs ago, but he had rallied under his nieces' loving care.

"Watch them well, Edward MacNeil," Stack had ordered in his rumbling voice just before they left Fort George. "They are my blood and most precious to me. I shall hold you to it now." He had adjusted his battered beaver felt hat upon his head and met Edward's eyes evenly. "You are a MacNeil, my boy, and so I trust you as completely as I do your father and uncle."

"Friendship is sacred to MacNeils," Edward went on. "You offer me friendship, but I cannot possibly return that offer if you continue to speak of Anne and Kate as enemies."

Paukeesaa brooded over this in silence for a few minutes. "I understand. They are the women of the Long Knives, but I will treat them with respect."

"The cave," Edward said suddenly. "I thought my uncle and my parents had told me every last detail about these islands, but they never mentioned that cave."

"It was not there until a few years ago," Paukeesaa told him. "The earth moved, just as my father said that it would one day. When it happened, the banks of rivers caved in on themselves and huge trees fell. In some places, one could not stand."

"I remember the talk at Fort George, but they had not really felt much there," recalled Edward.

"Nor did we," Paukeesaa said. "Yet the next time I came to this island, I found the earth had opened in that field. Until today it was known only to me."

"We shall say nothing of it," assured Edward. He gave Kate a stern, meaningful look. "Will we, Kate?"

"Not a word. But you did not answer my question." Kate was leaning up on her elbow. She had no knowledge of the code of manners amongst Natives. Brashness meant nothing, but a direct personal question could be taken as an insult. "Are you a half-breed? Your skin is almost precisely the same shade as Edward's. You both have the same sort of cheekbones and dark hair. Is your mother or father white?"

Edward gave a small groan; Kate was truly risking Paukeesaa's temper. Paukeesaa, though, simply gave her a condescending glance and said, "I am full-blooded Shawnee." It seemed to Edward that he was about to say more, perhaps name his father, but he did not. Paukeesaa lay down in silence and turned his face from them.

◇ ◇

The next morning was warm and still. Whatever animosity had filled the air the night before was gone. True to his word, Paukeesaa treated both Kate and Anne with polite deference. Anne lapped this up, chattering away to him in a manner that at first confused the young Shawnee, then amused him. He accepted it as one more bit odd behavior a Long Knife female might exhibit.

Kate insisted on examining his leg and although he clearly did not wish her to do this, she would not be dissuaded. "Do not move so. I shall be careful." Edward watched Paukeesaa thoughtfully staring at Kate as her cool fingers cleaned and redressed the wound. When she was finished and had moved away, he said to Edward under his breath, "She is your friend, but I still say she would make a good prize."

To Edward's satisfaction, whatever breeze had helped the sailboat to escape had died in the night. The lake was a flat stretch of glassy water; it would be a long, sweaty pull, but at least they would not have to fight the waves. Paukeesaa had only two paddles, and so he and Edward would use them. Kate and Anne sat in the middle, with Paukeesaa at the stern, where he would steer, and Edward at the bow. There was little talking. Edward slowly felt his muscles loosen as he dipped the paddle into the lake and pulled. Mercifully, the sky clouded over by noon so there was no sun beating down on them. Now and again, they heard the rumble of far-off thunder, but no storm came.

That evening they stopped on the mainland of Canada near the mouth of the Detroit River, for it made no sense to go all night against the current. There was only water and parched corn, but Paukeesaa waded into the sandy shallows and found a few freshwater clams. These he baked in the coals of their fire. It was enough to stop their stomachs from rumbling. Later he followed Anne while she walked up and down the beach collecting shells.

"We are but a day from my uncle's home," Edward told Kate. They sat near the remains of the fire. "There will be some way for him to help you get back to your parents."

"They cannot know that the ship has sunk. Not yet at any rate." She picked up a palmful of sand and let it sift slowly through her fingers. "That, at least, is a mercy." She dusted off her hand. "Are you certain it is only a day?"

"Oh, yes. I know the river very well. Paukeesaa and I will have to work hard to get us there. We will be paddling upstream, you see, but by evening we will be there."

Kate watched Anne for a while and then said slowly and uncomfortably, "I have been thinking about the promise you made to Uncle Elias. It was a great favor he asked of you. Tell me truly, Edward. Has it been a hardship for you?"

"Listening to such nonsense is the greater hardship," Edward answered in extreme annoyance. Then his voice grew warmer; she did seem terribly distressed. "See here, Kate. Elias Stack, my father, and Uncle John have known each other since before the war. Their friendship goes beyond time and distance, I think. I have known you and Anne for a mere fraction of that time, for only a year, but your companionship means as much to me. It is a pleasure and no hardship."

They both looked up when Paukeesaa gave a great shout. Anne was splashing him and his dignity seemed sorely affronted.

"I shall ask you again after you have the experience of spending a few more days in close quarters with Anne," said Kate. But she was smiling when she spoke those words, and Edward, who had not ever felt such a heavy weight of responsibility in his life, gave a silent prayer of thanks that she believed him.

◇ ◇

The next day was a very long haul. They passed a large island not far from the mouth of the river that Paukeesaa said was his home. He had lived there for many years with his aunt and her people.

"It is Grosse Isle, is it not?" asked Edward. Paukeesaa said it was.

"How can you know the river this well if you have not been here since you were a little child?" wondered Kate.

"My father and mother told me everything about it again and again," Edward said over his shoulder. "Uncle John wrote letters to me even before I could read them."

The MacNeils were passionate letter writers. Lord John MacNeil had sent great bundles of them back to England and Brierly each month on one British ship or another. As well as the long, rambling correspondence, there were sketches and paintings. Detailed maps of the river and Pêche Island had hung in Edward's rooms at home. Some of these he had brought with him. They are all at the bottom of the lake now, Edward thought sadly.

They passed Fort Amherstburg and the King's Navy Yard, and then the town of Sandwich. There were farms all along the water. The day grew hot and oppressive, and again far-off thunder rumbled. Slowly the wind began to rise and the river's surface grew choppy. By the time the canoe passed Fort Detroit, the American flag that flew over its walls was snapping smartly. Ahead of them the clouds were a dark purple. The storm hit just as they reached Pêche Island, and they struggled to pull the canoe onto the beach and into the shelter of the trees in the mounting wind.

"It is this way," called Edward. Already his clothing was soaked and water streamed from his hair. He led them through the woods and along a reed-edged canal. Raindrops slanted down, pocking the water and turning it a cloudy green. A great jag of lightning forked through the sky and an instant later thunder boomed. Edward thought briefly about another storm — the one that had brought his uncle to this island long ago as a boy. Then they left the wildly thrashing trees behind them and there was the house. Strangely, the door was wide open. They crossed the puddled yard and ran up the steps to the low porch.

"Uncle John," Edward called, but no welcoming voice cried out. The house was empty.

CHAPTER
FIVE

Edward stood there in the heavy silence. Although rain drove against the windowpanes, there was no sound inside the house. Leaves from the storm were stuck on the wide floorboards, and a chipmunk made a mad dash for freedom between Edward's feet. Kate pushed the door shut.

"Perhaps he is gone hunting," Anne ventured. She was trying to wring out the hem of her skirt.

"In this storm? Why would he leave the door wide open like that?" Edward's mind was whirling, trying to make some sense of this. He turned away from them and said calmly, "My uncle is capable of taking care of himself. I am certain he is not far and he will be back shortly. Besides, it was likely the wind that blew the door open." Kate looked doubtfully at the door's stout hardware. She made no reply.

Edward walked alone through each room; through the large room that looked out onto the river and lake, to the storeroom at the back, and then the pantry. He returned to where the others waited. Climbing the narrow staircase to the second floor, he opened and then shut the doors of the two bedrooms with their low, sloping ceilings. They were dim and quiet, the beds neatly made, clothing put away in chests and armoires.

Back downstairs, pausing hesitantly at the closed door of his uncle's library, he was too disheartened to do anything more than unlatch it and peer quickly in, for it was as empty as he knew it would be.

The storm had brought in cool air. There was tinder and firewood in the box near the hearth. A small silver tin on the mantel held charcloth and tow, a steel striker, and flints. They made a fire. Slowly the large room — a chamber Edward said was called the front room — began to warm.

Kate found hard tack and dried venison in the pantry. She found candles as well. They were all beeswax candles, finely made and redolent of honey. The storm was still too violent for them to venture out to the stone-lined storage room where more food would be kept, so with hot mugs of strong tea they made a plain meal. There was little conversation. At a loss for anything else to do, Edward showed Kate and Anne up to the bedroom where they could comfortably pass the night.

"I will leave this candle here. There is a pump in the pantry for water if you wish to wash. This was — is — my parents' bedroom. There will be some of my mother's night-dresses in that chest, I believe." He opened the chest himself. "Yes, just so. They will fit you."

"Will you not go to bed?" Kate asked. "You must be exhausted from the paddling." She shook out the linen nightdresses. Even after all this time, they still smelled sweetly of lavender.

"Where will you sleep?" asked Anne. She dropped to her knees and peered under the bed. "Good. A chamber pot." Kate rolled her eyes.

"Well, I slept here in a basket when I was a baby. I was never old enough to have a room of my own before we sailed to England. There is my uncle's chamber, I suppose. For now, I will sit by the fire for a while and wait for Uncle John to return. Sleep well."

Downstairs in the front room, Paukeesaa was cleaning his musket, carefully drying and oiling the metal. "Your uncle left quickly," he observed quietly.

"I know." Edward's dejection was total. "His musket is gone from the rack, but he did not take his document case. It is still hanging there as you see. He has always taken it everywhere so that he may sketch if he wishes. I cannot understand it." Edward pulled a chair close to the fire and sat.

In time, Paukeesaa stretched out on the old braided rug. "I will leave before dawn. The storm will be gone by then. I make my farewells to you now, Edward." It was the first time he had used Edward's Christian name. "Perhaps our paths may cross once again. It can happen in times of war." He paused and then grudgingly added, "Give my thanks to the girl Kate for her kindness."

Edward nodded. "I will walk with you to the beach in the morning. Thank you Paukeesaa, for helping us. I owe you a great debt."

Paukeesaa laughed softly. "I will make certain to

collect upon it." Then he turned his back to Edward and slept.

Edward fought to keep his eyes open, listening for the sound of someone coming home. There were only the faint noises of the fading storm, the gentle patter of rain on the windows, and the soft scratch of a mouse's claws as it crossed the maple floorboards. When he woke in the morning, the sun was just coming up. Paukeesaa was gone and Lord MacNeil had still not returned.

◇ ◇

Later that morning Edward took a musket, loaded it, found an old hunting bag and powder horn, and prepared to search every inch of the island.

"You will stay here," he told Kate and Anne. "Bolt the door behind me when I leave."

"What rubbish. You have a weapon. How could we possibly defend ourselves if someone comes? I cannot shoot at all. Besides, I thought this place was safe." Kate said in confusion.

"You must let us come along, Edward!" Anne insisted.

Edward regarded them. Kate was wearing an old petticoat and shirt of his mother's. It was clothing cut in the Native style, plain and practical, but the cotton was very fine stuff. She had a canvas bag slung over her shoulder. With her pale hair and fair skin, Kate looked rather odd. Anne had borrowed clothing as well, which hung loosely on her small body.

"It is perfectly safe, but this is wartime and I have no idea what has happened here," Edward replied, then surrendered with reluctance. "Very well, come along." He knew they would follow him anyway. Anne immediately rushed out the door to restlessly stand waiting for them on the porch. "I am not certain what we will find, Kate," he said to her in a low voice tinged with concern. "I pray my uncle has not been hurt."

Kate patted the canvas bag. "I have lint, clean bandages, and a tincture of laudanum I found in the pantry. There is a large herb garden behind the house. It is a bit overgrown, but I can see to it later. I will be able to make up poultices if I must." She touched his shoulder in gentle reassurance.

It was a lovely day, though unseasonably cool for July, and a fresh breeze blew from the Canadian mainland. Edward led them into the woods and up and down the beaches. Broken branches lay in the damp sand, and the trees showered their shoulders and heads with sparkling droplets. Ducks glided along the canals, and kingfishers hurtled into the water to emerge with small, shining fish in their beaks. They saw dozens of squirrels, and once Kate startled a rabbit, but there was no sign of Lord MacNeil.

Finally, they stopped in an old apple orchard, planted before John MacNeil had lived on the island. The trees were gnarled and in some places there were only stumps, for many had died and been cut for firewood. The dozen that remained were healthy enough, and, Edward saw, had many apples hanging from their branches. Off to one side his uncle, who lovingly tended this orchard, had planted a stand of very small trees; there would always be apple trees here, Edward knew.

Anne climbed into a tree and tossed tiny green apples down to them. Kate had cheese in the canvas bag. Edward nibbled at the tart fruit and thought of Brierly, for there was a small orchard there that had been planted from the seeds of these very trees. He felt a great, unexpected wave of homesickness, something he had not experienced for years. Suddenly it became very hard to swallow.

"What is this?" Anne asked. She was down on her knees in the grass. The timothy and wild oats had been clipped back here, from around a small rectangle of stone. Edward squatted down next to her and ran his fingers over the stone. There were no words and no one's name, which was odd, for it did seem to be a marker. Only a small dragonfly was carved upon it.

"I have no idea! Truly. We shall have to ask my uncle."

For the rest of that day they walked along the canals and down the beaches, going slowly around the oval-shaped island. It was only a mile or so long, and half that at its widest point, but Edward went deliberately. They spread out and walked through the trees and across the small meadow, calling for Lord MacNeil. There was no answer.

By late afternoon, they were nearly back to the house. "I will do it again tomorrow. There are some groves we passed by and perhaps he may be there." But Edward knew that his uncle was not on the island, that he had gone off for some reason.

"Look!" cried Anne. "A little boat!"

They had just rounded one of the island's points and were looking into a small cove. There was a white-painted sailing boat of perhaps fifteen feet floating not far from the beach in the wind-ruffled water. Another mooring in deeper water was empty.

"Why did I not look here first?" groaned Edward. "There should be another boat, the *Swift*, my uncle's sloop." He turned to Kate, filled with excitement. "He has taken the sloop and gone off somewhere. It is simply a matter of time until he returns."

"Might we sail, Edward?" begged Anne. "We need not swim out to the boat, Kate. We can easily wade."

"Tomorrow," Edward promised. He squinted into the sky with a sailor's practiced eyes. "This fine weather will hold for another day, I believe, and if so, we will sail out."

"We could sail home on this, could we not?" Kate asked.

"I would not wish to do so," Edward answered. "Think of the storm, Kate. A vessel this size could never stand against Lake Erie in a storm. When my uncle returns," he saw that she kept her features carefully blank at this, "there will be the *Swift*."

◇ ◇

The next day was clear; the wind had moderated a little and so they sailed all around the island twice before paddling the boat back into the cove and tying it to its mooring. During the next two weeks they sailed out now and again when the weather suited Edward. He had few ways to reassure Kate and Anne that his uncle would arrive any day. Kate said little, but quietly she worried. Her parents might have learned about the ship's sinking

by now and there was no way to get word to them. Edward
tried to distract them and himself.

Kate took to sailing immediately. She learned to trim
the sails and to steer. Anne coiled lines and took her turn
at the tiller. All worn out with fresh air and soakings
from waves that splashed against the hull of the boat, the
three of them slept well.

One night however, Edward, could not sleep at all. He
sat alone in the front room by a low fire, rubbing the
wolf's head pendant between his finger and thumb.
Finally, he picked up a lamp and walked to the back of the
house. The door to his uncle's library was closed. Since
their arrival, Edward had not entered the room again.
Now he lifted the latch and went in. He used the candle
in the lamp to light several others, and slowly the library
filled with soft light.

A window looked out toward the north. Edward knew
that would give his uncle the best light for painting if he
worked inside. Scores of books stood on high shelves;
the room was a library as well as a room in which to paint.
There was a desk of cherry wood. Edward saw his own
letters there, letters he had written months ago. Had
Uncle John read them one last time before he had left?
Looking them over, Edward felt his throat tighten.

Where there were no bookshelves, there were paintings. One study stood unfinished on an easel. This is me!
Edward thought in amazement. He came closer and
examined the portrait carefully. John MacNeil had
caught the steady gray eyes, the dark plait, and the elegant shape of Edward's face. The skin looked as smooth

as a girl's. That much is true, he thought, rubbing his cheek. He would never have anything resembling whiskers growing there; it was the legacy of his Native blood.

The figure would be dressed as a seaman in a shirt of blue ticking and trousers of heavy cotton when the painting was completed. But those things, and the background, were sketchily rendered. Only the face was finished. It was to be a surprise, Edward was certain of this, and it made his heart ache.

Sketches lay in rolls and piles, and on the walls were many paintings. Each had a tiny brass plate to identify the person. Edward saw his mother and father, younger versions of his parents, but them nonetheless. There was a childhood sketch of his Aunt Jane holding an odd-looking dog. Here were his grandparents, stiff and dignified; his grandmother in a formal Court gown, his grandfather in his red captain's uniform. Edward's eyes widened in astonishment. This certainly was Marie Roy, the childhood friend of Lord MacNeil. Edward's father had told him about this painting. Paddling a canoe that was just about to disappear into the mist, she was smiling brilliantly.

The room should have been sad, for so many of these people were gone now, but it was not. It is like looking back in time, thought Edward. I have heard about all of them and listened so often to the stories of what they did. I wish I might have known them all.

Then he saw the painting of three people that hung over the mantel. It was no larger than the others were, but it seemed different somehow. A silver locket was draped over one corner. He stood there lost in thought, gazing upon their faces. There was a small noise behind him. Startled, Edward turned around. It was Kate.

"I woke and could not get back to sleep. I came down to borrow a book." She crossed the room. "Who are they?" she asked in a soft voice. A large shawl modestly covered the nightdress she wore. She stood on tiptoe to read the names on the brass plaque.

"She was Charlotte Wolf, Charlotte MacNeil Wolf, for she took the name of her husband's clan as her wedded name. He was Owela, my mother's brother. The little boy was their adopted son, Thomas," Edward answered. He had not needed to look at the names, so certain had he been. The painting showed a young woman of perhaps nineteen years. She wore a long dress of golden yellow and her chestnut hair was held back in a simple club. A wampum belt of white beads with blue dragonflies worked down its length hung over her shoulder. The Native at her side was tall and serious; the little boy mischievous. Behind them was a forest, deeply shadowed and green.

"They are dead then?"

Edward nodded. "They called her Mack. She was not only my aunt but also a distant cousin to me. She was Uncle John's ward, as was my father, when they came here to stay with him as children."

"How did they die?" whispered Kate. "They look so young."

"It was during the Revolutionary War," Edward answered. He lifted his shoulders. "That is all I know.

My father and mother would never say anything about it and Uncle John said little more, but I know they all loved each other very much. I have heard many happy stories about them and all of the adventures they experienced here. I always thought that my parents wished to remember only those happy times."

"They do look very happy."

Edward reached out and ran a finger across the painting. "I think their deaths changed my parents' and Uncle John's lives forever. I am certain that is why my father — and Uncle John especially — hate war so intensely and have little use for the military. Not war itself, they have always said, but what it does to people who have no wish to be touched by it. Uncle John made his peace with it all long ago, he once told me, but somehow I cannot believe it."

"What a sad thing," Kate said. She stood very close to Edward. "It is just as you say," she began. "War will come closer and closer until we are in the midst of it. I have thought about this and I must ask that you take us to Fort Detroit, Edward. If my parents and Uncle Elias have learned of the ship's sinking, they will be grief-stricken. We must go to them immediately."

"But you know no one at Detroit, do you?" Edward asked gently. Kate shook her head. "You cannot simply wander the streets hoping someone will take you both in," he reminded her.

She began to twist the end of the long braid that hung over her shoulder. "I have thought it out. We will go to the commanding officer and ask for his help. Perhaps there will be a ship that is sailing to Sandusky or somewhere nearby. Until I can arrange to book passage on one, I can find work of some sort. We must remove ourselves from this island, since it is part of Canada."

"I understand. I will take you if that is what you wish," Edward said reluctantly.

That night in his bed, he lay awake for a long while. He was not accustomed to being solitary. Brierly had always teemed with cousins and visitors, and the *Marie Roy* and *Odonata* had been crowded and happy. If Kate and Anne left, he would be alone. I am not certain how I will like that at all, he thought, but I must bear it.

The next day they set out for Fort Detroit. It would be an easy voyage, not so many miles, and the current running downstream would help them along in the light wind that blew.

An hour later Kate said, "That is strange. I can see no clouds and yet I hear thunder. I know well by now how unpredictable these waters are, but is a storm coming, do you think?"

Edward was peering hard at the shore, his face serious. "A storm of sorts," he answered slowly. "That is the sound of cannon, and, if I am not mistaken, it comes from Fort Detroit."

CHAPTER
SIX

When Fort Detroit was in clear view, Edward could see that a white flag hung over its walls and the Union Jack was flying. He heard cannon fire and the higher pop of muskets. Smoke drifted in the air above the walls.

"It is a flag of truce." Kate's voice trembled. "What has happened?"

The fighting was over. The noises they heard were the sounds of celebration, as the captured artillery was fired and the muskets of the Native allies discharged.

No one opposed Edward and the girls when they neared the fort's water gate. American soldiers, now prisoners of war, were already being loaded into boats.

"What has happened here, sir?" Kate asked a young officer.

"Move those men along. They are prisoners, not guests," the officer called out. Then he looked down at Kate and Anne, mistaking them for locals. "You, miss, and the girl must go back inside. You interfere with the business of the Crown!"

"Lieutenant, that is uncalled for," Edward said. "We are interfering with nothing, sir."

The lieutenant's eyes widened a bit at the young man's clipped accent. This was no Canadian or even a common sailor, in spite of the clothing he wore. With a bored sigh the officer said, "Fort Detroit has surrendered with barely a fight, upon my soul. These soldiers will wait out the war as our prisoners in Quebec." Then he turned back to his task.

Exchanging incredulous looks, Edward, Kate, and Anne slipped past the officer and entered the fort. For the first time in seventeen years, Detroit was once again in the hands of the British, for the American General Hull had, indeed, surrendered to General Brock.

A very old man stood by the gate, watching the proceedings with keen, bright eyes. "Quite a sight it was," the old man told them in French without being asked. Edward spoke French but this patois was most odd. Edward concentrated hard to understand as the old man talked rapidly. "In they came, marching in a row, their fife and drum playing some English song. They took down the American flag and ran up their own. What a sight!" Edward translated the news for Kate.

"What will happen now?" she asked. "None of this makes sense!"

Edward could scarcely understand the wild scene himself. It did not seem like anything he dreamed of when he thought of war. Natives, armed and painted for battle, ran up and down the streets shrieking their war cries each time a cannon boomed. British solders not engaged in the transport of prisoners cheered as well. Some of the townspeople were crying. A boy with a fiddle played a wild tune, and a group of girls were dancing with their young men.

"It is something, eh?" laughed the old man. "They say no homes will be touched. It is only the soldiers they will take away for their prison ships. We who have always lived here will just live on. One army is much like another, eh? I have seen them all come and go. French, British, American, and now British again. This is war, *mes amis*. It is not supposed to make sense!" He cackled heartily at his own joke and wandered off to enjoy the spectacle.

"I will not leave either of you here," Edward said firmly. "The fort is in British hands. The military will never help you, Kate. You must both come back to the island with me." He could not bear to see her stricken face and the way she clenched her hands.

Anne, though momentarily worried, soon let it all drift away. Things would fall into place one way or another as they always did. She looked around curiously, smiled with mischief at a passing soldier, and then shrieked, "Paukeesaa!"

For it was Paukeesaa. His face was painted black from his hair to the bridge of his nose. He was armed with musket, knife, and a deadly looking tomahawk. His eyes narrowed when he heard Anne's greeting, and then he turned his back on her. Anne would not be ignored though, and she pushed through the crowd to face him.

"Go away," he hissed. Paukeesaa looked past her toward where half a dozen warriors stood. He grasped her shoulder, turned her around, and gave her a push. "I have no wish to be seen with you."

"You do not sound pleased to see me," Anne called over her shoulder.

"My word, Paukeesaa!" grumbled Edward. He rushed forward and took Anne's hand. "It is only that she is happy to see you." Edward turned from him, disgusted with Paukeesaa's behavior, and walked straight into someone. The man, a Native, held Edward away from him with one powerful hand and they both examined each other.

The Native was tall and well built, and, unlike many of the other warriors here, dressed in an older fashion. He wore a shirt of doeskin and a sword belt of morocco leather. Long leather leggings and moccasins completed his garb. His powder horn was plain and unadorned; it was clearly a tool rather than something worn for a special occasion. He carried a musket, and both a tomahawk and a knife were at his waist. Long and loose, his hair hung to his shoulders.

The Native's grip on his arm was steady, but Edward had the distinct impression that its owner felt a keen revulsion at the contact. Edward met the man's regard evenly. He felt a cold rush of fear, but somehow he knew that if he showed one bit of that, it would be most unwise. Then the man smiled, the incident passed, and he released Edward. Edward looked around to see that the armed warriors were hovering near him, poised to strike out if need be. The man said something. They all laughed grudgingly and stepped back.

Paukeesaa's entire being drooped. The man looked at him pointedly and Paukeesaa drew himself up as well as he could. He said something in his own tongue. The man's brows lifted and he answered Paukeesaa in a rough voice. Then he looked over to Kate and acknowledged her.

"He says to pass on his thanks for what you did to help me," Paukeesaa said woodenly. "He said you, Edward, were unflinching, that you would be a good one to fight alongside in battle." Paukeesaa would not meet Edward's eyes.

"Battle?" wondered Edward with a short laugh. "I have not ever been in battle, and I do not hope I shall experience it soon. How might he have thought to say so?"

"Who else might be more qualified to make such a judgment?" Paukeesaa laughed humorlessly. "He is my father, Edward. He is Tecumseth."

Edward had heard of the man at Fort George. They said Tecumseth was a Shawnee chieftain who had done more to unite the Natives than any other had since Pontiac. Tecumseth's influence had brought all these warriors to fight alongside the British. It was the strength of his will and the power he had over people that had done it.

Edward could not take his eyes from the big Shawnee, so strong was his presence.

He did not hear the cries through the town; the sound of cannon firing held no more meaning than the snap of an impatient girl's fingers. He stood there and thought, I would give a good deal to see my uncle draw that face.

Tecumseth had strong features. He was handsome in a

way that Edward had not often seen. His skin was a dark bronze, far darker than his son's. High, sculpted cheekbones, a finely arched nose, and a mouth that gave little away in spite of its appealing smile. Then the eyes, deep and calculating. Locked in their gaze, Edward had at first thought them to be friendly, inquisitive, but no, that was not it at all. He had only experienced intense dislike a few times in his life, for Edward was likable and liked most people. That is it, he thought. It is pure loathing I see there. He wondered why. Then he thought of the loathing in Paukeesaa's eyes.

"Tell him that it was my pleasure to help you," Kate said, tired of being ignored.

"And tell him we must leave and return to Pêche Island," Edward added.

Paukeesaa repeated the words in Shawnee. Tecumseth smiled again and said, "Now and again it calls to me, as well. The elders say that Pontiac would go there to pray for wisdom when he had a great decision to make. Many spirits live there. Do you know this?"

"I do," Edward offered after Paukeesaa had translated. "My uncle has told me the stories. I am not surprised. Pêche Island is a peaceful place."

"Your uncle?"

"John MacNeil." Edward did not add that his uncle was not on the island. He hoped that Paukeesaa would not include that detail.

"I have heard of this man. You must give him my greetings. He is like me. Some of us are men from another time, are we not? But those times will come again. Another occasion then, for we will be here, more and more of us, until the war is won and the lands that were ours are ours again."

"Another occasion."

"And perhaps you may pass time with my son. Paukeesaa is no warrior. He is all but useless in battle and does not even look like a Shawnee with that pale skin of his, but he is here with my men." If the rage in his father's eyes was carefully hidden, it was not hidden at all in Paukeesaa's. The young Native was livid with fury at his father's words, but he repeated them in an uneven voice.

Tecumseth snapped something at his son and then turned to the British officer who had just arrived. Edward heard the name Brock spoken but he had no time to look at the man, for Paukeesaa had taken his arm and was pulling him away in a painful grip. Kate and Anne followed.

"He says I am to see that you are safely away. I will do it. I am no warrior, you understand, but I can do this," he muttered bitterly. At the water gate where the boat was tied, Paukeesaa turned to Edward. His eyes flicked over Kate and Anne. "Go then and take your sister with you." Kate did not move. Her arm was around Anne. Paukeesaa looked down. "Go, I say, Kate. It is not safe for you here and Edward will protect you." He lifted his hand when she began to protest. "Do not say you can care for yourself. Perhaps you can, but this is war. There is no mercy in war."

"Take care, Paukeesaa," Anne piped up.

For the first time he smiled at her. "I will, Anne." Kate

did not speak, but she gave Paukeesaa the ghost of a smile. Then she walked hand in hand with Anne through the crowd at the water gate toward the boat.

"It has truly begun now, has it not?" Edward asked. He saw the shame on Paukeesaa's face at his father's shabby treatment and he wished to steer any more of their talk away from it.

"The British have taken Fort Michilimackinac and there has been fighting at Brownstown. Both were victories for my people and their allies. There will be more until the fight is done and the lands owed to us are ours once again." Paukeesaa followed the girls' progress as they walked away. "You and they said nothing to my father of how we met, that I was cowering in a cave while others fought." The words came painfully. "He thinks little of me. He would think less if he ever learned of that." He looked back at the fort and went on. "Do not let Kate and Anne try to reach their home. They will surely be slaughtered."

Edward felt his scalp crawl at the thought. "They will be with me until I can see a way to get them to their parents." He clasped Paukeesaa's hand and the other did not pull away. "You hate whites, you say. Well, I am no white. I am not Native and not really an Englishman since I was born here. I think perhaps I have no idea yet of what I am. You need not waste your time in hating me — or the Kimmerling girls, for that matter. You are welcome on the island whenever you choose to come there." He released Paukeesaa's hand and quickly strode away.

The journey back to the island was quiet and solemn.

Kate was stunned at what had passed. She could not think clearly about what she must do. Anne only watched the birds and gulls that flew overhead, for she was most fond of all creatures. Edward felt a slow dread building within himself.

It was evening by the time they moored the boat. Anne splashed into the water and went ashore. Edward looked away when Kate pulled her skirts well above her knees and slipped over the side to walk slowly to the beach.

The house was just past the line of maples and high bushes that edged the sand. A clear walkway had been trod out, and they went back without talking. Edward lifted the latch and walked into the house. A figure sat in a chair by the hearth. Uncle John! Edward nearly cried, but the fellow was far too young to be his uncle.

"Who are you?" asked the young man, with his hands on a musket. "How dare you set foot in Lord MacNeil's house?"

CHAPTER
SEVEN

Edward and the girls stared at the young man. Before they could say anything, the stranger spoke again. "We heard that someone had moved into Lord MacNeil's house in his absence and I said to myself that it would not do at all." His English was heavily accented. He would speak French normally, Edward supposed, or rather the local patois. "Lord MacNeil is generous to a fault and will help anyone, but to take from a man when he cannot defend what is his, I call that low. Low indeed. Who are you, and what are you doing here?" But before Edward could defend himself, the fellow slowly stood, peered at him, and said, "I know you, I do, but I cannot put a name to you."

"I am Edward MacNeil," Edward said faintly. "And you?"

"I am Pierre LaButte! By the bells of Ste. Anne's, you are not drowned at all!" Pierre set down the musket, crossed the room, and clasped Edward's hand. "You have the look of your uncle, and of your father and mother in the paintings John has done.

"Ah, me, what a thing this is," he went on. "Word came from passing Natives that the vessel had sunk and all aboard had perished. They had found a sea chest with *Patience*'s name on it floating in the water. The news nearly killed your uncle. Not any argument my father used would stop him. He tried to reason with him — we both did. My father even tried to hold him back, but John was like a man gone mad. He said he must be alone and he would not even say where he was going. He cared nothing for the fact that there is war and that it would be foolish for him to travel on his own."

Edward went to the window and looked out onto the lake. What pain his uncle must have suffered. "Where did he sail?" he asked tiredly.

"Out to Lake St. Clair and then probably north to Huron. But he will return, Edward," Pierre said with certainty. "This island has always been a refuge for him."

Kate rushed to Edward's side. "He thought you were dead. And my parents must believe the same thing has happened to us. News surely must have reached them. We must try to get home, Edward." Frantically, she turned to Pierre. "Would you take us to Ohio, sir?"

"Ohio?" laughed Pierre. "*Mademoiselle*, there is war all around the lake and raiding parties everywhere. You might be killed or worse."

"What could be worse than being killed?" asked Anne with great curiosity. Though Kate blushed deeply, she did not answer her sister.

"There is food in the pantry and fresh squirrel meat hanging in the cold room," Edward said heartily, trying to lighten the mood, for he could see Kate wilt with disappointment. "You will stay the night, surely, Pierre. It is my pleasure to meet you at last. Uncle John wrote often of you. He has always said that there has been a close bond between the LaButtes and the MacNeils since he knew your great grandmother Marie long ago. He sent sketches and if I had not been so surprised at seeing you, I would have known at once who you were." Edward took a deep breath and forced himself to smile a little. Where is my uncle? he thought desperately as he walked to the door.

"Edward, you must not look for him. He will return when he is ready," said Pierre, understanding what Edward was thinking.

"I would have no idea where to look." Edward glanced over at Kate and Anne. Both were clearly fighting panic at the thought that he might begin the search. "I will not leave," he assured them. "A few hours alone, if you please."

Carrying his musket, Edward left the cabin and walked to the cove. His heart was beating very hard and his throat was tight and painful. He waded into the water, set the musket in the boat, and climbed in. He began to untie the painter and then he knew he did not wish to do even that, so he lay back and pillowed his head upon a folded sail.

Edward lay there for a long while. The moon rose, slightly fuller than half and wreathed in low, filmy clouds. Bats shot back and forth across the stars. Frogs and insects sang their ancient songs from where they hid. Edward felt that he might weep for loneliness, but, of course, he could not. A young gentleman would never weep. He did not feel the tears that dripped down his face as he slept.

When he awoke, the moon was well up. Pierre was standing in the water, his folded arms on the boat's rail, his chin upon his arms. "I need your help," Pierre said with desperation.

Edward sat up. "What has happened?"

"The *mademoiselles* began arguing when you left and have been hard at it since. Do they do this often?"

"Now and again," Edward told him wearily. He dipped his hands in the cool water and scrubbed them over his face.

"Like my sisters. And like my sisters they turned on me when I tried to separate them."

Edward splashed into the water and together they waded ashore. "Kate, the older one with the long blonde, hair, she worries for her sister's safety and her parents' piece of mind. It is no more than that I think."

The house was quiet when Edward and Pierre returned. They heard a door slam on the second floor and then all was silent once again.

◇ ◇

In the morning, Edward expected Kate to plead and beg, to make a dreadful scene, but she did not. Instead, she said, "If we must stay here, then we must, but might letters be got to them somehow?"

"There could be a way," Pierre answered thoughtfully. "The Natives travel where they wish with no thought to boundaries. There is always someone crossing the lake or journeying around by land. A private letter, you understand, with no reference to anything regarding the military. Otherwise, it would be thought treasonous and if anyone was caught carrying such a letter, it surely would be his death. My father would be the one to arrange to send such a letter, and I know he would insist upon this."

"I will let you read anything I write," offered Kate.

Pierre laughed aloud. "I do not read English. It must be Edward who does so."

Edward felt a hot flush creep up his neck. He did not care for this at all, for reading her letters would violate her privacy. But it was war. It is changing everything, he thought. "Yes. I can do that," he said reluctantly. Then with more warmth in his voice, since he could see that she was as embarrassed as he was, Edward said, "Write your letters, Kate and Anne. Would you all excuse me, please? I have one of my own to compose." Pierre bowed and moved discreetly away from Kate, as Edward went up the stairs to his uncle's bedroom.

Kate looked around for a place to write. At one of the windows in the front room was a table with paper stacked upon it in neat piles. There were swans' quills in a blue glass vase and a small knife for sharpening them. Bottles of ink, sealing wax, and a roll of red ribbon lay there. Kate pulled out the chair, sat, and picked up a sheet of the paper. It was heavy stuff, much finer than anything she had ever seen. What must it have cost? Her family had nothing to spare for such expensive things. With a deep sigh, she uncorked a bottle of ink, picked up a quill, dipped it in, and began. Anne followed her sister to the table. She stood next to Kate to write, her face screwed up in concentration, the tip of her tongue poking out from between her lips. When Edward quietly came down the stairs a quarter hour later, Kate had just signed her name. She held out the letter without a word. Edward read aloud:

"Dearest Mama and Father, both Anne and I are well and safe. Our vessel went down in a dreadful storm and many were drowned. Only Edward MacNeil and we survived. You will recall Edward, as I mentioned him many times in letters home to you. We managed to reach the safety of South Bass Island. A less than companionable Native, whom we came upon there, brought us to an island in the Detroit River not far from Fort Detroit.

"We are here at the home of Edward's uncle, Lord John MacNeil. Edward says that Lord MacNeil will in time find a way of helping us to return to you. There is war between Canada and the United States, as you must know. They say it is not safe to journey. This surely being so, you must not try to come to us here.

"We are safe and among friends. Edward MacNeil is a gentleman. He has read this letter, as he must, to make certain nothing in it could affect the course of the war.

"It will be easier for you than I to get word of all that has passed to Uncle Elias. Give him our love.

"I shall think of you every day until we are all together once more. With love from your devoted daughter, Kate."

"Now mine," Anne said stoutly, handing him a rather splotched sheet.

Edward read:

"Dear Mama and Papa, I am well. Kate is well. Edward has a fine boat and I will become a sailor some day. I have a Native friend called Paukeesaa. Please do kiss Kerry for me. Love, Anne."

"Kerry?" Edward puzzled.

"Yes, Kerry," said Anne with indignant wonder. "Surely you remember my mentioning him. He is our dog."

"Of course," Edward said. "Who else might it be, but your dog?" He turned to Kate, who at least now had a little smile on her lips. "You must read mine, for it is only fair."

Kate took the sheet from him and with Anne peeking over her shoulder, she read Edward's letter:

"Dear Mr. Kimmerling, I assure you that as long as your daughters are within my care, I shall do all I can to protect them. As well, I will do what I must to arrange their safe return to you in Ohio. Until that time, they shall come to no harm here and will be treated with respect and courtesy. Your most humble servant, Edward Wolf MacNeil."

"There is this as well," Edward said quietly. "It is a letter for my uncle. He could be anywhere — Georgian Bay, Manitoulin — there are a hundred islands and coves in which he might anchor. If he chooses to hide himself away, it will be difficult to find the *Swift*, but I must try to send word that I am alive."

"Of course you must," Kate said, gently touching Edward's arm. She turned to Pierre. "You will send someone out quickly, will you not?"

"Canoes and bateaux come and go each day," Pierre explained. "Your letters will reach their destination in time."

But perhaps mine may not, thought Edward. I cannot be certain mine will reach Uncle John.

Edward folded the letters and tied them up with red ribbons. He lit a candle, melted sealing wax upon the ribbons, and pressed one of his uncle's seals into the red blobs. He handed the letters to Pierre, who slipped them inside his shirt.

They walked together to the cove where Pierre's canoe lay in the bushes. Edward helped him carry it down to the water.

"Are you coming back?" Edward asked him.

Pierre gave him a smile. "Indeed, *mon ami*. I am not needed at the farm at this moment. There are many hands there to do the work, what little there is until harvest. But you, Edward, will need a great deal of help." Pierre looked sideways at Kate and grinned impishly. "Besides with me here, you have a better chance of surviving life with these two females." He gave the canoe a shove, leaped in, and picked up his paddle. "Be brave until I return, my friend!"

CHAPTER
EIGHT

Pierre returned to the island in a week and Edward was most pleased to have his help, as well as his company. They were each in their own way used to hard work — Edward at sea and Pierre on a simple farm — but neither had ever taken on the entire responsibility of readying a household for winter. The weather was fine, but once fall and then cold weather set in, there would be a hard price to pay if they were not prepared. There was wood to cut, the garden to weed and water, all the unending work of running a household. Tasks fell into a natural pattern. Kate and Anne worked in and around the house — Kate took charge there and soon the house was clean and ordered to her liking. Edward and Pierre took on the heavier outside chores. It was a way of life that Edward found satisfying.

Outwardly, the two young men had little in common, but still they slowly became friends. Their coloring was much the same; both had dark hair and tanned skin, but there the similarity ended. Pierre was the son of a Métis farmer, for generations ago his ancestor had wed a Miami woman. He was tall and well muscled, a happy, outgoing person. His Native blood was unimportant to him — so many here were a mixture of French and one tribe or another. He spoke a rough patois that was nothing like Edward's Court French, and his English was oddly accented and peppered with strange expressions. They made jokes about how mismatched they were, but daily their friendship grew.

There were only squirrels and rabbits to hunt on the island, and Edward did not wish to kill too many of these. Instead, they took ducks or a goose. There were mallards, pintails, canvasbacks, and the beautiful geese of Canada. They set a fish trap in the lee of the island and once went out for deer on the mainland.

There was a smokehouse. The smaller game they ate fresh, but Edward and Pierre cut the venison into pieces and hung them in the smokehouse where hickory chips burned in a low fire. Some of it they salted in small brine barrels and then hung in the cold room in flour sacks to keep away the flies. It was hot, sweaty work, but if the hunting was poor this winter, they would still have some meat.

Often in the late afternoons, Edward and Pierre would swim. When they were alone they stripped unself-consciously to their skins and left their clothing on the sand. Most of the time, however, the girls were there with them, Kate wading on the beach and Anne furiously splashing about in deeper water in a heavy shirt. In spite of her fear of the water, Kate eventually waded deeper and deeper until, with Edward's help, she tried a few tentative strokes. The afternoon that she swam from the beach to the boat and back again was a great victory for her.

Pierre had a fiddle. "Someone in my family has always played," he explained. "My grandfather, Pierre LaButte, taught me and I will teach my own son some day." His music was like nothing Edward had ever heard before. Some of the songs were so melancholy it brought tears to their eyes. Others were wild and merry — they could not help but stamp their feet. Kate or Anne would drag Edward up out of his chair sometimes, and they would dance while Pierre played.

It was a time of waiting. Slowly the nights grew cooler, September began to work its changes upon the trees and meadows, and still Lord MacNeil did not return, nor did a letter come from the Kimmerlings. They did not speak of this since talking about it would make them worry even more.

Now and again, a passing local brought word. There was the horrifying news that the Native allies of the British had been raiding all around the lakes. Pigeon Roost Creek, Fort Harrison, Fort Madison, Fort Wayne were all attacked. In October, two British vessels were captured at Fort Erie by the Americans, and at Queenston Heights General Brock was killed.

Edward had found a small bag of coins in his uncle's bedroom, but he did not wish to spend any of them. All their purchases had instead been recorded against Lord MacNeil's account at the trading post at Amherstburg; the proprietor knew that the bill would be paid in time. Captain LaButte carted the supplies to a spot just across from the island. Then Pierre and Edward brought the bags of cornmeal, flour, salt, dried beans, and other goods across by canoe. Edward and Pierre also brought news to the girls that Pierre must go home to help with the harvest. Pierre's father had been firm about this.

It was a dull afternoon. Cold rain came down in sheets onto the sandy beach. Edward did not wish Pierre to leave, but could not protest, since family came first. "You are a good friend, Pierre," he said with feeling. "I could not have done all this without you." There was now plenty of firewood stacked against the house, and a good store of smoked meat, root vegetables, and flour in the cold room.

"You could have. Those two know a great deal about keeping a household in running order. Either will make a fine wife for some lucky fellow some day." He laughed at the look on Edward's face and slapped his shoulder. "I leave you in their hands, Edward!" Abruptly, he grew serious. "You will not reconsider? I do not like the idea of leaving you here when winter comes. It can turn very harsh at any time and it would make it that much harder to get to you. We LaButtes are crowded at the house, but we would make room for you," coaxed Pierre. "Kate and Anne would enjoy the company of my sisters and even my brothers, and I would not be deprived of yours, Edward."

Edward reluctantly shook his head. "Uncle John may return." He looked off across the lake as he said this, not wishing to see the pity in his friend's eyes. "I must be here if he does."

But Lord MacNeil did not return. November came

and went, a sad, lonely month of bare trees and dismal, leaden skies. Edward walked the beach each day, looking for a sail in the distance. The weather turned brutally cold and snow fell steadily. Storms whipped across Lake St. Clair and drifts banked up against the side of the house. Edward and the girls carried ticking and quilts from the second floor and moved into the large front room so that they could sleep near the hearth.

One night, Edward lay awake staring at the low flames. Tomorrow would be Christmas Day. An arm's reach away, Kate and Anne slept peacefully, bundled together under the heaviest down quilts. Outside the wind roared. Edward sat up and pushed away the bedding. The girls wore nightdresses; sometimes they each wore two against the cold, but Edward usually slept in his clothing. He took a candle from the mantel, lit it, and went to his uncle's library.

There was no fire burning here and he could see his breath. He held up the candle so that he could study the painting of Mack and her family. It was then that he really noticed the book that lay on the mantel. A wampum belt of blue and white beads worked into the images of dragonflies, lay across it in graceful folds.

Edward slid the book from beneath the belt, brushed the dust from the cover, and read the initials engraved in the leather. CWM. Of course, it must be Mack's journal. Seated in his uncle's chair, heedless of the cold, Edward read for a very long time. He stopped once to light a second candle, but other than that he did not pause.

At first, the entries were perfectly happy. The journal

had been a wedding gift from John, her guardian. It told of the joyful marriage, the small longhouse that Edward's father, Jamie, and John helped them to build. They had chosen a spot on the lake for their home. Akiksibi, it was named. Later they built a log cabin. There were journeys to Fort Niagara and farther to a place she called the Oneida Castle in New York. It was a fine life, rich with promise and the love of their families. That happiness would soon be greater, since Owela's family had made the decision to join them at Akiksibi. The Americans had burned the villages of Natives who were allies to the British; it was only a matter of time before retaliation rose against the Oneida and Tuscarora.

Then, the Revolutionary War, which they always believed could not touch them here in Canada, exploded into their lives in the form of an Oneida runner, near dead with exhaustion, who had come as quickly as he could from Fort Niagara.

1 February 1780
A Native came to our cabin this dawn with the hardest news. With other Oneidas, Owela's parents, Alex and Nì:ki, and his dear sister Sarah, left the Castle. Senecas, who bear the Oneida no love these days, set upon them. The Oneidas drove the warriors off, but Alex has been badly wounded, and is perhaps by now dead. They reached Fort Niagara for they could go no farther and cannot come to us. With hundreds of others, Owela's family huddles outside the walls of Fort Niagara finding what shelter they may.

We argued in a way we never have, more hotly than when we first met. Owela would have sent me on with the runner to John and Jamie at Pêche Island. I refused to leave him. Neither would Thomas go. We are strong and fit and easily kept up on snowshoes, taking turns helping him pull the toboggan toward the fort. The day was long and cold, so very cold. My bottle of ink had frozen in my pack and I had to set it near the fire before I could pen these words when we stopped to camp.

5 February 1780
I will not write again until we reach Fort Niagara. We are weary beyond belief. Last night Owela whispered to me that although he wishes I had gone to the island and kept Thomas with me, he is so very grateful I am here for the comfort it gives him. I pray John and Jamie are not far from us.

Fort Niagara, 1780
I am not certain of the day. Alex Doig died of his wounds this morning. I fear Owela's mother will not live until dawn. She is so weak. There are many dead outside the fort's walls, all frozen or starved. There is no food to share with them and, having been driven out, their longhouses burning, they did not even have time to gather blankets or provisions. There is no firewood. They have burrowed into the snowdrifts as have we, pressing close together against the cold.

I was recognized. The ward of Lord MacNeil must come inside and take shelter, they said. We will make room for you and give you hot soup. But there was no room for Owela or his mother. Thomas will not leave his father. He is the finest son I could ever have had.

I did not wish to go inside, but Owela insisted that I do so. I could not refuse him. The officer said I might bring in the child if that would get me within the protection of the fort. She is small, he said, and it does not look as though she will live anyway. He spoke of Sarah, Owela's sister. She is thirteen years old and so much reduced by hunger that even I can carry her. She is sleeping now, poor child, having eaten up the soup they gave me.

I will go back out. Sarah is safe and warm here until we return for her. They say the storm is fierce and may be the worst yet this winter. Let all who read this know that I have not been forced to leave the fort. It is my choice and I make it willingly. Owela is my husband and whatever shall happen, whenever it happens, we shall be together.

One does strange things at times of crisis. The morning we left, I stuffed the wampum belt I wore on my wedding day into my pack. I will wear it now, for the dragonfly is Owela's totem and mine. Perhaps it may give us strength.

John and Jamie have not come yet, although I know in my heart they will.

Here the handwriting changed from Mack's elegant script to one more plain. The words were shaky at first, but grew clearer and stronger as the writer struggled to express the painful thoughts.

29 March 1780

This is not my journal. I would not think to write within it, except that I knew its owner well, and care for her and her kin deeply. It seems to me that this journal is like a book, and someone else — a friend — must add the last page to the story lest it go untold.

Charlotte MacNeil Wolf, whom they call Mack, her husband Owela, and their son, Thomas, all died in a terrible storm at Fort Niagara, February 1780. Many others died as well, their bodies are still frozen in the drifts and embankments outside the fort. There they will lie until soldiers may cover them in lime and bury them all together. Some already call this The Winter of Hunger.

John and Jamie MacNeil were too late. It was by chance alone I met them in the lower town and learned of what had passed, but by then there was no hope, for one of the worst storms of the winter was raging and no one outside the fort could survive. Had I known of Mack's presence here, I might have helped. I will regret this to my dying day.

We might not have found their bodies until spring, but the smallest piece of her wampum belt showed above the snow. MacNeil and his brother dug them out with their bare hands so frantic were they. I fear John MacNeil may not paint again. His fingers were badly damaged.

John and Jamie were near mad with despair and grief. The only thing that sustained them was the girl Sarah. They nursed her most tenderly in the lodgings I

*found for them in the lower town. John MacNeil will
not set foot within the fort ever again. His rage against
the military is great.*

*Sarah is strong enough to travel and the weather is
decent. John and his brother will take the sad remains
home. He says they will build platforms so that the bodies may rest under the sky in the Oneida way. In time,
there will be a single grave in the apple orchard. There
is enough snow to use toboggans. I will travel with them
as far as the mouth of the Niagara River.*

May they find peace, both the living and the dead.

I remain your most humble servant, Elias Stack

"Are you ill, Edward?" It was Anne, flushed and
sleepy, wrapped in a quilt, her eyes bleary without the
spectacles. She chafed her cold feet one against the
other. "Oh, Edward, you have been weeping. What is
it?"

She crossed the room and kneeled in front of him.
How deeply he cared for her friendship, he suddenly
realized, her warmth and lightness of spirit.

"Only a very sad story," Edward said. He pulled her to
her feet, set the journal back on the mantel, and rearranged
the wampum belt across it. "Back to bed, Anne. It is
Christmas in the morning."

They settled in their nests again, but Edward did not
close his eyes for a long while. He thought about the
marker of stone that lay out in the orchard covered in
deep snow. He no longer needed to ask his uncle about
it. Mack, Owela, and Thomas rested there beneath the

dragonfly, their totem. He thought of choices and bravery. When at last he slept, he did not dream at all.

In spite of the restless night, Edward rose early with Kate and Anne. The evening before, he would have fired a musket into the sky to celebrate Christmas Eve, but the brutal storm had held him back. Instead, he stepped outside today, coatless, and fired his Brown Bess into the cloudless day. The echoes died away. In the forest a woodpecker tapped, the branches of the big old trees creaked in the wind, and sunlight sparkled in the fallen snow with unspeakable beauty. Christmas morning had arrived.

There were small gifts. Kate had sewn a shirt of fine, creamy linen for Edward and a lovely new dress for Anne from a bolt of cloth she had found upstairs. Anne had knitted scarves for everyone. Edward had woven each of the girls a turkshead bracelet from heavy marline — one with two strands for Anne and one with three strands for Kate. That they had sat together in the evenings working on these things was not important.

It was pleasant and happy at first, but then clouds moved in and the sunshine faded. The day became cheerless no matter how hard they tried to make it merry, and that afternoon Edward was certain he could hear the sound of weeping coming from Kate and Anne's room. It was cold on the second floor, but Kate had sought privacy there; Edward stood outside the doorway, wretched and alone, unable to offer her any sort of comfort.

Finally, he simply went back down to the front room. He stood staring out the window, barely seeing Anne, who was rolling a ball of snow with little success. It was too cold and dry for the snow to stick together. Edward turned at the sound of Kate's footsteps coming down the stairs. She had washed her face and although her eyes were red, she gave him a warm smile.

"Let us put on all the clothing we can find and take a walk," Edward suggested desperately. "Anne is outside already."

Bundled in cloaks and heavy stockings, each with a warm knitted muffler and mittens, they were an odd sight, for the outer clothing was that of a time gone by. There were but two pairs of snowshoes, so Edward and Kate strapped them on.

Out into the cold they walked. The snow was deep in places and so they tried to make a path for Anne; finally, though, they left the woods behind and stepped out onto the beach. Here the sand was swept nearly bare of snow. The wind blew very hard and flakes pelted their faces. A new storm was just roaring in from out on Lake St. Clair. Snow fell heavily, hiding the horizon and the mainland.

Edward peered out intently as he always did. I cannot give up hope, he thought wearily, much worn out from worry. A harsh blast of wind cleared the blowing snow — there was someone on the beach! Edward's heart gave a wild leap. Had his uncle come at last? But then another gust of wind parted the veil of snow for a moment. "Pierre!" called Edward. "What on earth are you doing here in this weather?"

It was too noisy and crowded at home, Pierre told him. His cousins had pestered him to death and his sisters would not cease from chattering all at once. "It will be far more peaceful here, and so I thought I would come across and help with your Christmas celebrations." He had rowed across in his father's wooden bateau, for the canoe was too light to risk the ice floes that drifted everywhere now. "That is, if you will have me?" he asked hesitantly. "I would not wish to intrude."

"Of course!" cried Kate.

"It will be great fun!" Anne agreed.

"You could never intrude," assured Edward, slapping him across the shoulders. "I will help you beach the boat and stow the oars and we will return to the house." Then in a lower voice he said, "It is so very good to see you."

Pierre picked up his musket which had been lying wrapped in oilcloth in the boat. He fired into the air once. A few seconds later, an answering shot came from the mainland. "My father said that I must signal him when I reached here," he explained. "Not that he could do anything had I tumbled into the river."

There was a great deal to carry, for Pierre's mama would not let him come to Lord MacNeil's island empty-handed — especially on Christmas day, for the love of all that was holy! She had sent *tortierres* of veal, venison, and pork, as well as fresh bread and a *tarte* of last fall's apples from the island. Pierre had his fiddle, wrapped in a case of canvas. There was even a small *traine*, a sled of about five feet, made of thin, birch boards.

Pierre strapped on his snowshoes, and told Anne to sit on the *traine*. They piled everything on it and set off. Edward and Pierre pulled the sled together while Kate followed.

By the time they arrived back at the house, the storm was in full throe: the wind was shrieking and pellets of snow battered the windowpanes. They were lonely sounds, but the flicker and crackle of the fire, Kate and Anne's happy faces, and Pierre's cheerfulness muted the gnawing dread that ate at Edward. Was his uncle safe and warm in this horrible winter weather?

"And now for the best," announced Pierre, once they were in. "There is a letter here from your father, *mademoiselles*." Yanking off one mitten with his teeth, he reached inside his coat and pulled out the letter. They both screamed with joy to see their father's familiar handwriting on the paper.

Edward wanted to ask, What of my uncle? Is there any word of him at all? But he did not. Pierre would have offered news immediately, and he did not wish to spoil the girls' happiness. Instead, he squeezed Kate's hand, patted Anne's shoulder, and said heartily, "I am very happy for this."

Kate's attention was on Pierre. "Please. Let me have it," she insisted anxiously.

Pierre still held her letter. His face was red with the cold, but it turned redder still when he had to say, "My regrets, Kate. My father insisted upon opening your letter to ensure my safety since I was carrying it." The room fell silent. There was only the pop of wood burning.

"Of course. I understand," Kate said stiffly. She took the letter. The seal was broken. The folded paper was plainly tied with coarse string, she tugged it loose and carefully opened the letter.

"Read it aloud, please," Anne begged.

They pulled off their coats and cloaks. Edward tossed a log onto the fire and said, "Let us sit here where the light is better."

With Anne at her feet, and Pierre and Edward warming their haunches at the fire, Kate began to read aloud:

"My dearest daughters, I suspect that this letter will have been seen by eyes other than yours before you read it. If that is the price we must pay, then so be it, for we are so very grateful to Edward MacNeil. Your mother wept bitterly when news came of the ship's sinking. She wept tears of joy to hear that you are alive and well and under his protection."

Anne stood and went to her sister's side. Together they read the news from home in silence. Kate looked up and smiled. "Thank you so much, Pierre."

Pierre bowed elegantly. "It was my pleasure, and it has put you in a good state of mind, so you will be prepared for the next thing I must tell you."

"What is that?" Kate asked suspiciously.

"When the weather allows, you are all to return to the mainland with me to either stay with my family or at Fort Amherstburg. My father insists. The war grows hotter and at least the fort and town are well defended."

"But we are Americans," fretted Kate.

"It is a British fort," Anne said. "It will surely be the prison for us. Bread and water. Fleas. Rats! Dungeons!"

"Do not worry," said Pierre, throwing out his chest. "I

myself will defend you if you choose to brave the company of my family." Under his breath he added, "You especially, Edward. I have many sisters, after all."

"And if we go to the fort, Pierre?" Edward asked shortly.

"My father said that he would make all arrangements for you there," Pierre assured him.

For Edward it was a bittersweet evening. There was teasing and laughter, Pierre's fiddle music, and even dancing, but behind it, he felt the ache of longing for his uncle.

Much later, Anne was yawning and so Kate lit a candle and led her upstairs to the bedroom. Then she came back down for several quilts. "We will be warm enough bundled up together, and, if not, we will come back down. I know you two wish to talk." She paused at the foot of the stairs and, without looking at them, said, "Sleep well, Edward. I have some fear for our safety at Amherstburg, but the truth of it is, I would rather remain here peacefully with you." A deep blush that Edward could see even by candlelight rose up her neck. She turned to Pierre and said, "It is so fine to have you here once again." Then she walked quickly up the stairs.

Pierre and Edward sat by the fire for a long while. At first they did not speak at all; clearly both enjoyed the silence after the happy commotion of their reunion. Then Edward leaned forward, picked up a chip of wood, and tossed it into the flames.

"Are they saying that he is dead?" Edward stood up and walked to the window. A great sigh of wind rushed through the trees. Nothing was visible, for the storm's clouds hid the moon.

"There is no word at all," Pierre answered slowly and with great reluctance. He stood and walked over to Edward. "That means nothing. You know as well as I do, Edward, that if your uncle wished to be alone, no messenger with a letter would ever find him. And if your letter did reach John, he will know you are alive. It is likely that the *Swift* is frozen in the ice. With the weather as bad as it is, your uncle is not fool enough to try to return."

Edward put his face in his hands. "I cannot lose heart. Until I see his body with my own eyes, I cannot despair." I am so very close to it, he thought, swallowing back the tears that threatened. Then he said, "Let us go north, Pierre. We will take the girls to your family and then set out to find him."

"My father was certain you would say something like this. It is partly why he wants you away from here."

Edward bristled at this. "He is your father, Pierre, not mine. I am under no obligation to obey him."

Pierre laughed aloud. "He said you would say that as well. Edward, he could not bring the news himself, since the militia is on alert. He trusts me to bring you back, and he trusts me, really trusts me, with little. He will not even let me fight. I will be sixteen years old this time next year and of age to join the militia and fight with him. Until then he will not permit it." All this came out in a stream of frustration. "What I would have given to have been at Fort Detroit when he and my uncles helped to take it. Even you and the girls saw more than I did, for you were there!

"He treats me like a boy and he will do the same with

you, and it is no use arguing. Your uncle is his dear friend, and my father has assumed responsibility for you. Do not think to escape him. War or no war he would find you and bring you back."

His misery forgotten, Edward sputtered with anger. "I am no boy, Pierre. I have been on my own for years. Well, as much on my own as one can be aboard a ship. I have also taken care of these two for many weeks."

"Kate would be cross to hear you say that," chuckled Pierre. "I wager she thinks she runs this household." His face grew serious. "We have time here together, Edward. We cannot go anywhere until the weather breaks."

The weather did not break, though. A winter colder than any Edward had ever known gripped the country-side. Although his faith in his uncle's skills as a woodsman was strong, Edward wondered if anyone could survive. There was no question of leaving. It was not so much the distance. Pierre's home and farm were almost directly across from Fort Detroit, and Pêche Island was only a short way from the mainland, but the high winds and the ice floes that churned the river's surface would make a crossing treacherous. If Edward had been alone with Pierre, they might have tried it. Edward, however, would not risk any harm to the girls.

They settled in, locked within winter's frigid grip. Kate sewed endlessly, pulling apart old clothing to fashion new dresses for herself and Anne. She made trousers for Edward and Pierre while Anne knitted scarves and stockings. There were long games of draughts or cards during which the girls intensely debated the rules.

Once, when a temporary lull in the fierce wind permitted, they walked out to look at the stars. Edward had been delighted to find a small telescope in his uncle's library. From his time at sea, he knew the stars very well. The telescope would be perfect for what Edward wished to show his companions.

"There in the east is Venus, and there, to the southwest, is Jupiter," he explained.

"How lovely they are," Kate murmured, peering through the glass. "They say you can see Jupiter's moons if the glass is powerful enough."

"Look just to the right of it. You will see one." It pleased Edward deeply to hear her soft laugh of pleasure.

A few times, they tried a game of lacrosse. Anne had found an old leather-covered ball and four sticks wrapped in canvas, tucked away in the rafters of the pantry. It was a wild, rough game; both Kate and Anne played with a fierce abandon that left Edward and Pierre rattled.

"They are rougher than the Natives with whom I have played," puffed Pierre, rubbing his shins.

They stayed out as long as they dared, but even stuffed with rags, their shoes and moccasins were not adequate. The knitted caps were also not enough. Pierre suffered a touch of frostbite on his toes and the tips of Edward's ears were badly nipped, and so they kept to the house. Kate fussed over them, seeming almost pleased to have someone upon whom she might practice her healing.

The river froze over, and in February, Captain Julian LaButte walked across. Pierre and Edward snowshoed out to meet him.

"He is pulling a *traine*," Pierre said. He waved his arms over his head and his father lifted a mittened hand in return. Pierre began to run with the odd lurching gait needed for snowshoes.

Edward was less enthusiastic. All he knew of Captain LaButte was what he had read in letters from his uncle. To this had been added Pierre's stories. In spite of the fact that his father was a hard, strict man, Pierre clearly loved him very much. For him this would be a happy reunion. For Edward it would mean subjecting himself to the wishes of his uncle's friend.

LaButte was a big man with dark hair and bronze skin. His features told of the Native blood in his veins far more clearly than Pierre's did. He embraced his son and then seized Edward's shoulders and embraced him as well.

"You do well enough, I see, in spite of this weather. It would be easier at the farm, you know," suggested Captain LaButte, in heavily accented English. But he did not intend to force the issue — at least not today. "You are secure enough here, at least until the spring," he told them as they walked back to the house.

Once inside, LaButte stood at the fire warming himself. "There is no fighting here at the moment. It was brutal at Frenchtown last month. You would not think they would be so foolhardy to plan winter campaigns in such weather, but war and the British military care not a thing for that."

Edward saw a weary man, bone tired of both hardship and killing. "Is there any news of Uncle John?" he asked.

"None," came the answer. Captain LaButte scrubbed

his hands over his face. "How old are you, Edward? Fifteen? Yes. Like my son here."

"I will be sixteen years this summer. I am old enough to look after myself, sir. I will not be forced to return to your farm. This is my uncle's home. If he is dead — and I have faith that he is not — I am his heir and it is mine. I will defend it just as he would have."

"And I will help him," Pierre said boldly. It was the first time he had ever dared defy his father.

Julian LaButte's dark eyebrows lifted at his son's boldness. "I will not force you, Edward. Nor you, Pierre, but you must remember your responsibilities to our farm, my son. All the signs say that we will have a long winter and this cold will continue, but when spring does arrive, you must come home, Pierre. And I advise you to think carefully before you choose to remain here alone with these girls, Edward." Kate and Anne were in the pantry putting away the supplies that LaButte had brought.

"I have accepted the responsibility of watching over them, Captain LaButte," Edward reminded him. "I will not shirk it."

LaButte sighed. "Of course, you will not. But it would be far safer in town or at the fort. Besides, there is talk."

"What sort of talk?" asked Kate. She was carrying a pot of cider to set over the fire. Behind her, Anne had a tray of mugs.

"The women gossip, as the women in our village always have," Captain LaButte said in an offhand manner. He glanced at Anne.

"I am no baby!" Anne protested. "Do not think to

send me out of the room if there is something bold you must say."

"Two unwed females are living at Lord MacNeil's house with his nephew and my son. It is most scandalous," explained LaButte. "Think of their reputations, Edward, if you and Pierre care nothing for your own." He held up his hand when all four of the young people began to talk at once. "Understand I do not share in this. I am confident that you, *mademoiselles*, are out of harm's way in the company of such capable and respectful young men as Edward and my son."

"We will stay on here for a while longer, Captain LaButte," Edward said firmly. "As you see, Kate and Anne are content."

"We are most content, sir," Kate said firmly. "If we cannot return home, then my sister and I will stay with Edward."

"But what of us, *Père*? What of Edward and myself? Who will protect us?" asked Pierre. He fell to his knees, clutching his father's shirt. To Edward's relief, everyone laughed, the tension evaporated, and there was no more talk of leaving the island.

CHAPTER
NINE

Many months later, on a cool, foggy dawn in early July, Edward guided the sailboat down the Detroit River. A gentle breeze blew. Wreathes of mist hid the shore and there were few sounds except for the hiss of the hull through the water. Dew dripped from the rigging. At his insistence, Anne and Kate sat sheltered under a tarp so that they would stay somewhat dry. He wore oilskins, but they were old and soaked through.

Damp and miserable, Edward ran a hand over his dripping hair, and then firmly grasped the tiller once more as a sudden gust filled the sails. He had put off coming here for as long as he could; finally, Captain LaButte's entreaties had won him over. That, and the fact that they were building a ship at the Navy Yard at Fort Amherstburg, had broken down his reserve. It was hardly news to the locals. The vessel had been under construction for some time, but Edward had paid little attention at first. Then, when the island slid from winter's icy grasp and they could again sail again, he felt the idea of the ship calling to him.

Fort Amherstburg was just ahead, ghostly in the mist. Sentries, soldiers of the 41st Regiment of Foot, walked along the earthworks. The British flag hung limp and heavy from its pole. Many Natives stood or crouched, weapons in their hands, watching as the small boat approached. Below the fort was the town of Amherstburg. Edward thought he could just make out the warships tied at the wharf near there.

"I am heading her up into the wind," Edward called. "We can make the pier easily." Kate nodded but had nothing to say. It had been a quiet voyage. She was sick with worry at the thought of being an American at a British fort while this war continued, but she would not have parted company with Edward under any circumstances — Anne for once agreed with her sister and was strangely silent as well. Kate threw off her part of the cover and stood. She would not let him do this on his own.

"For pity's sake, Kate, you will catch your death," said Edward hopelessly. She stood close to him, squinting at the fort. "Please do not be so fearful." He touched her hand. "Not a thing will happen to you here. You and Anne will be treated well. Captain LaButte has given his word." He began to say something about his uncle's influence, but then he stopped. "I am a MacNeil," Edward explained instead. "It does mean something here."

"Pay her no attention, Edward. I will watch out for Kate," Anne piped up.

"You hush!" Kate snapped. "It is all a game to you, Anne."

"It is no such thing," Anne argued. "I did not wish to

leave the island any more than you did, only I choose not to show it."

"Quiet, the pair of you, and help me here or we will run right up onto the shore," Edward said testily. Their arguments were mindless, born of closeness and the fact that each was as independent as he was. It was a daily, sometimes hourly, occurrence so he should have been used to it, but he was tired of it at this moment. "There are Captain LaButte and Pierre," he called with a cheerfulness he did not feel, and both their heads snapped around.

Anne began to wave furiously, Kate moved forward, and Edward pulled the tiller. In a sweet, smooth motion the boat turned up, the sails flapped, and she bumped softly against the small pier.

"You are here at last," cried Pierre.

Captain LaButte caught the line that Anne threw to him. "Well done and welcome!" he cried. "Lord MacNeil could not have done better."

Edward cast a hard look at LaButte, but the man was smiling widely at the girls. He had meant nothing at all by the remark, but it cut at Edward somehow. I am not my uncle, he thought suddenly. I am Edward Wolf MacNeil.

Something fell away from him at that moment. Some weight of responsibility, the endless, impossible heritage and all the stories that tied him to his family — what did any of that matter now? He was alone here and he was his own man.

"Come quickly to the barracks, Kate and Anne," Captain LaButte said warmly. "There is a fire in the hearth and hot soup. You as well, Edward, for you are all as soaked as muskrats. I will help you with your belongings. Whatever is in this chest, now?"

"My uncle's things," Edward said shortly. "I could not leave them there. The house is closed up. The furnishings and clothes do not matter so much, but I could not leave his work." He cleared his throat and added, "There is a letter at the house for him, in case he comes before I return to the island. Then he will know where to find me."

The night before, Edward had penned the note and set it on the table by the window in the front room. His uncle could not miss it; he was certain of that. Alone in the library, he had spent hours carefully removing each painting from its frame, stacking papers, letters, and any document that seemed important. Finally, he gently picked up Mack's journal, the locket, and the wampum belt. All these things were now inside the small chest.

The LaButtes had come down in a wagon pulled by an old workhorse. "I will take this to the house then, Edward, if you wish," Pierre's father offered. When Edward silently agreed, unable to express his thanks aloud, LaButte put the trunk in the back and covered it with a tarp. Then they started out for the fort.

"You are positive that you will not return home with us?" Pierre's father asked bluntly. "You are welcome there and it might be better for you, Kate and Anne. It is not so far. Only a few hours away."

"I thank you, sir, but no," Kate said immediately. "We will remain with Edward."

"You would have to help with the late planting. A very intelligent refusal," Pierre teased.

"I would happily help you, but I will not leave Edward," Kate repeated firmly.

Inside the barracks, a fire crackled in the hearth. The long room was filled with off-duty soldiers eating a late breakfast. Heads turned only slightly when Captain LaButte walked in; he was well known to them and had led his militia regiment in all the battles fought in this area. He did not command any of these soldiers, for they were enlisted men, but he had their respect. A man called out to Pierre and a few questioning looks were cast Edward's way. When Kate and then Anne entered the room, though, a silence fell. Someone gave a low, meaningful whistle and Edward felt anger rise inside himself.

Understanding very well the nature of these common soldiers, LaButte said only, "This is Edward MacNeil, the nephew of Lord MacNeil. These young women are under his protection. I know I may expect that your behavior be of a gentlemanly sort." The MacNeil name caused a change in the air. A man fetched bowls and spoons; another pulled chairs to the fire.

"I have known your uncle since I was a boy," one old soldier said. "A fine man."

"Brave and true," said another. "And a good friend."

"He won't be dead at all, either," called out a man, and Edward winced.

"What a thing to say," grumbled the old soldier. "Never you fear, lad, Lord MacNeil is too smart and tough an old bird to simply wander out into the bush and die or let his ship sink under his feet."

"There is a small house nearby that you may have," Captain LaButte said to Kate. "It is enough for the two of you." He turned to Edward. "Commander Barclay arrived just last week. He knows you are here, Edward. Do not be surprised if you are called in to see him."

Edward could see the discomfort in Kate's manner. He knew how she fretted about being here and how reluctant she was to part from him — especially here. "Captain LaButte," Edward said in firm voice. "Is there nowhere within the fort that Anne and Kate may stay?"

"Camp followers?" called a boy, and he laughed with loud braying howls until someone smacked him alongside the head.

Edward felt his heart go out to the girls. He began to speak in their defense, but Kate shook her head. "I take no offense." Her cheeks were flaming, though. She stood there, her hands on Anne's shoulders, as unruffled as she could make herself seem. They both wore fresh, clean gowns of sprigged cotton; Kate had done everything she could to make both of them seem respectable, given the gossip of which she was aware. "There is no shame in being a camp follower, in baking and washing and mending. Molly Pitcher followed her husband during the War of Independence and carried water to the men on the battlefield. It was a different time and a different country, but she is no less a heroine for it."

"We have empty tents you may use, miss," one soldier offered. "They are spoils taken from Detroit, but no one will mind." LaButte nodded his approval.

"Have a care, my girls, lest you find yourselves taking the King's shilling," another laughed.

Kate looked across at Edward, clearly confused. "Enlisting," Edward explained. "Joining the army." His voice was even and he was grateful for the hospitality they were showing them, but in his head he thought, I would never do any such thing. It would go against every wish my family has ever had for me. But what of my wishes? he asked himself. Alone now, with no one to say what he may or may not do, Edward was no longer quite so certain of what he wanted.

That evening Pierre and his father prepared to return to their farm. As they made their farewells, a red sun was just disappearing behind the lacy leaves of the trees on Bois Blanc Island, just across the water from Fort Amherstburg.

"I will come back when the last of the late crops are planted and I am released from the slavery of farming," Pierre promised. He gave Anne a great, smacking kiss on the cheek, clapped Edward across the shoulders, and, bowing to Kate, said, *"Au revoir, Mademoiselle Kimmerling."* He climbed into the wagon next to his father.

They waved until the horse and wagon disappeared from their view. "Why did he not kiss you good-bye?" asked Anne innocently.

"It would not be seemly," Kate answered with her nose in the air. "You are a little girl. I am not."

"A little girl!" cried Anne and the arguing commenced

in such a boisterous and familiar way that Edward was nearly happy to hear it. They chattered and picked at each other like squabbling birds while they helped him pull the tents into order and lay out the pegs so that they might pitch them just beyond the fort. The house that Julian LaButte had offered would certainly have been more comfortable for the girls. Edward was pleased, though, that they had chosen to camp with him.

They had been provided with small wedge tents, comfortable for one or two, though while on campaign a half dozen men would squeeze in. The tents were stained and worn in spots but they would not leak — at least not much. From somewhere Captain LaButte, surrendering to the will of the Kimmerling females to remain close to Edward, had found them more bedding, a pot, and a few kitchen implements to add to what they had brought from the island. There was day-old bread and some cornmeal for mush. The next morning, Edward could walk to the trading post for other supplies. He knew, however, there might not be much to be had. With all of the Native allies in the area and the needs of the military, goods were in short supply.

"Captain LaButte said that they would happily share what they can with us. Pierre will bring things from the farm in time, fruit and vegetables and such," mused Edward. "They say Uncle John's name is enough, that anything we purchase will be credited to him, but it would be simpler if we had more money. The bag of coins I brought from the house will not last long."

"I have money," Kate said very quietly. Edward felt no

anger that she had not said something before. He knew how hard life was for her family and whatever coins she had been given would be saved until there was no option but to spend them.

"She is the rich sister and I am the poor one," Anne laughed. "She never spends a penny. I would give it all to you if I had some, Edward, but I cannot seem to keep even a single coin in my purse."

That night they sat near the small fire that was left from preparing their plain food. The sky was star lit. Only a wisp of cloud floated across the moon that hung low over the trees. Kate was inside one of the tents, laying out the blankets they had brought with them from the island. She had carried a lantern in with her. Edward thoughtfully watched the movement of her shadow on the wall of the low tent. He saw the fine line of her profile for a second. Her long braid swung as she bent forward to smooth the bedding.

"She worries all the time, you know," Anne said suddenly. She was sitting very close to Edward in her companionable way. Her hands were cupped around something. She smiled a sweet smile, pushed back her spectacles with her forearm, looked up at Edward, and carefully opened her hands. A small cricket crouched there, the first Edward had seen this season. "There is not a thing you may do to change that, Edward. She worries enough for all three of us. Leave her to it." Anne set the cricket in the grass and it scrambled away. "She is horribly homesick. I miss Mama and Papa dreadfully — and my dog, of course — but Kate can hardly bear it, I think."

"I care for her, Anne," Edward quietly told her. "She has become like a sister to me. You both have."

Anne leaned her head against Edward's shoulder for a moment and then sat up. "I have no brother. You shall be my brother. I will miss you, Edward, when we are home again. Kate will also but she will never say so." She looked at him out of the corner of her eye. "Since she is not the little girl she says I am."

Kate pushed the tent flap aside and said, "Look here, Edward. I have had this sewn into a small purse on my shift all the time we have been away." She sat down near him, her legs crossed, and from a cloth pouch poured the small hoard into her lap. There were pennies and half pennies and three half crowns. Edward saw French coins as well, a few three livres. He thought of Brierly, the large estate, the carriages and servants and comfort. How odd it seemed now.

"Excellent," he said. "Tuck it away again, Kate. When we need it, I will let you know." He would rather starve than ask her for the money she had so carefully guarded.

"What we have is surely yours, Edward." Kate put each coin back in the pouch, smoothed her hair, and stood. "All is ready, Anne, and it is late enough. Come to bed now. Tomorrow will be very busy."

Anne climbed to her feet. She must be very tired, indeed, to be going without an argument, thought Edward. Anne waved good night to him over her shoulder.

"Sleep well, Edward," Kate said, then she let the tent flap drop.

Anne lay down directly, but Kate sat and began to

unbraid her hair. Edward could see her shadow as she ran a comb through it with long, slow strokes. When she rose to her knees and began to pull her dress over her head so that she might sleep in her shift or change to a nightdress, his face grew hot. He knew he must turn his eyes away. She trusted him above all else and he would not betray that, even in secret. Letting out a breath he had not even known he was holding, he stared out across the river.

Low words came from the tent and Kate sputtered, "For mercy's sake! I did not even think of it!" He could not help himself and looked, but the tent wall was dark, for someone had put out the candle.

"Good night, Edward," Anne called out cheerily, and then there was only the sound of the girls' muffled giggling. Edward might have been cross, for surely they had found him out. Instead, he felt a strange sort of relief, for it was a very happy sound in this decidedly unhappy place, and when he lay down to sleep in the other tent, he thought perhaps he had made the correct choice in coming to the fort.

In the late morning, they walked past the fort to the Navy Yard. Edward had only gone over to watch, but the smell of newly cut wood and the sound of the adzes and hammers moved him. He had long enjoyed working with his hands, carving and building. His years on the *Marie Roy* and *Odonata* came back to him, for above all he loved to do any sort of work on a ship.

With great desperation, a balding man grumbled to the officers who stood next to him. "Imbeciles. Fools and dolts with no more skill than apprentices a day into it. She will never be finished at this rate, and then where will we be with not a hope for victory? Why, we will be up one creek or another, and not a prayer to be had for a paddle at all, much less a ship!" He wrung his gnarled hands. Then he screeched, "Have an eye there, you blockhead!"

The workers ignored him. Many were *habitants* from up the St. Lawrence and spoke little or no English.

"Now, Mr. Bell. She will be finished," soothed Commander Robert Barclay. "You are the Master Shipwright in charge of the King's Navy Yard. If anyone is capable of pulling it off, Bell, that man is you."

Edward saw a fine-looking young officer, very spit and polish and British Navy to the core. One of the sleeves of his uniform coat was pinned up — he had lost an arm in battle, Edward would later learn.

"She is larger than I thought she would be," Edward murmured.

"What's this?" boomed Bell, seeking a fresh victim. "Have you a commentary? Of course, she is large! What do you know of it at any rate? I am surrounded by experts it seems."

"I am no expert, sir. I have worked with wood. I often assisted the ship's carpenter when I was aboard our vessels."

"Carpenter? Your vessels?" asked Bell eagerly. "What's this now?"

Barclay watched with an assessing eye.

"My father's and uncle's ships, actually, sir," Edward explained. "*Marie Roy* sailed from Plymouth to Halifax for three years, and then I served aboard *Odonata* on Lake Ontario." Kate and Anne stood quietly near him as he explained.

"*Odonata*," murmured Barclay. "A merchant vessel, is she not?"

"He would be Lord MacNeil's nephew, Commander Barclay," reminded the other officer. "Captain Julian LaButte sent word of his possible arrival, as you certainly recall, sir."

"Ah, yes, Lieutenant Garland. So this is Edward MacNeil." Barclay nodded thoughtfully. Then he gave a graceful inclination of his head. "Welcome to Fort Amherstburg, young MacNeil. What do you think of our ship?"

"She promises to be a fine vessel, sir," Edward answered.

"See here, lad, can you cut and saw?" Bell grumped.

"Aye, sir."

Bell looked down his nose. "Can you hammer a treenail home straight and true?"

"Indeed, sir! I can sand, and lay a plank, and set in oakum properly. I can rig when it comes to that job."

"You are the man for me, then, MacNeil. Go to the barracks there. You will find the sergeant major and the doctor somewhere about. They will judge you fit for service, or I will know why. It's a fine day to join the 41st," laughed Bell.

"Mr. Garland will hear your oath of allegiance to His Majesty," Barclay added absently. He turned his attention to the ship.

Edward grew very still. "I will not do that, Mr. Bell. I

would surely enjoy working with you and for you, but I will not join up. I will not fight."

"Are you a coward, then?" someone called out from where men worked on the *Detroit*. They had been listening to the exchanges.

"Perhaps his loyalties are confused," called another. "British or Native. How will it go?"

Edward clenched his fists, longing to seek out the men who had shouted those words. Instead he calmly said to Bell, "I am at your service, Chips, sir." This was the name given to all ships' carpenters and although Bell was far more than that, the word had come into Edward's mind.

Bell slapped his thigh and laughed aloud. "You are a sailor, my boy. I have not been called that for many a year. If you can do all you say, I care nothing for whether or not you will fight on this boat. There will be little if any pay, mind you."

"I do not want or need your money," Edward answered in a cool tone, although inside, his wrath was smoldering. His words were careless, but the idea that notice had been taken of his skin rather than his intentions cut deeply. He looked sideways at the girls. Anne's expression was troubled, but Kate was furious that he had been so insulted.

"Oh, it ain't my money," laughed Bell. "It would be the King's money, God bless his soul."

"What of your companions?" asked Garland. He was younger than Barclay, fresh faced and open. "These would be the American girls, the Kimmerlings, then? At your service, miss." He made a courtly bow over Kate's hand, and Edward felt an absurd rush of jealousy.

"I am Anne and she is Kate," offered Anne, keeping her own hands well behind her back.

"What date might this be, Lieutenant?" asked Kate.

"Why, it is July 4, 1813, miss."

"Independence Day. How odd." She glanced up at the warship and gently pulled back her hand. "There will be fireworks back home in celebration. Independence is a treasure, Mr. Garland. Come, Anne. We must see to dinner." She looked at the men one by one. "Good day to you, sirs."

"She is a haughty one," laughed Garland. He watched Anne and Kate walk away. "As cool as can be."

"Sir, she is not haughty at all, only fearful of her acceptance here under the circumstances. You are, after all, British officers, and at war with her country," Edward answered briskly.

Barclay's eyebrows lifted. "*We* are at war? I do beg your pardon, young sir, but if I am not in error, you are a British citizen. It is your war as well." He pulled his waistcoat straight with his one hand, smoothed back his hair, and settled himself. "See here. We are not inclined to make war on young women, Mr. MacNeil. Our country is at war with theirs, but I assure you, their well-being is not to be questioned."

For a moment, everything Lord MacNeil had told him about the military and navy came into Edward's mind: the sense of duty to the Crown before anything else, the promises broken to expendable allies, the brutality. This was a harsh place and a savage time and if Kate and Anne were to be defended, he must leave nothing to chance.

"I do not question your honor, sir. Yet, if you give me your word on this, then you have mine that I will help Mr. Bell."

Barclay stiffened. Then he mastered his irritation at this puppy's nerve, for they sorely needed the skills of one such as Edward MacNeil, even if it was in an unofficial capacity.

"You have my word," he drawled. "Mr. Garland, you will let it be known that if any soldier or sailor approaches the Kimmerling ladies, there will be a high price to pay."

And what price will I pay if I help build this ship? wondered Edward. But he only said, "I will return shortly, sir. I must reassure Kate and Anne."

Barclay and Garland watched Edward break into a run as he followed the girls.

"Interesting, is he not, sir?" Garland said.

"Quite," Barclay admitted. "The nephew of one Lord MacNeil, you say?"

"Indeed, sir. Captain LaButte — he is attached to the militia here — says that Lord John MacNeil is a man of tremendous influence at Court. He is still referred to as the King's own artist in Canada. Apparently, it is some sort of unofficial position he has held since he was a boy here at the end of the French and Indian War. Most eccentric, I would venture, living almost like one of the Natives and even at times amongst them."

"The nephew has rather the look of a Native, it seems

to me, but he sounds like a young lord," Barclay observed. "He could be useful, Lieutenant. See if you may enlist him to do more than simply pound treenails."

"I shall. My pleasure, sir," Garland promised.

◇ ◇

When Edward reached their camp, he learned that a man had put a letter directly into Kate's hands only moments ago. At the sight of her mother's handwriting, she had torn it open and read it. Now she sat in the grass in front of her tent, her eyes glassy with unshed tears, the letter loosely held in her cold fingers.

Edward dropped to his knees next to her. "Kate, what is it?" he asked gently. "Your mother and father. Is all well?"

She looked at him with a great sadness. "Mama has written."

"Oh, pray read it aloud, Edward," Anne begged unsteadily.

Anne put an arm around her sister. Kate stared out down the river toward where the lake and their home lay. "Papa is just like you, Edward. I have often thought so, although I have not said as much. You both have strong views. Neither of you can admit this, preferring to appear detached, but you are fiercely loyal. And you each have the same skill with wood! I should have known what would happen. How perfectly cruel this is."

Edward took the letter from her and read aloud:

"My dearest Kate and Anne, I must tell you that your father is no longer at home. You are both old enough to understand the marks that the War of Independence left on all of us. There was not a family we knew that was left untouched.

"It happens again. He will not fight, he says, and yet I cannot be certain he means this."

Their father had known his duty, the letter went on. He was an experienced shipwright, and so he had journeyed to Presque Isle, east of Sandusky on Lake Erie, to help build the ships that would become Commodore Perry's fleet. They must pray for their father and for all the brave sailors, both American and English, who, in time, would man the ships and fight what would be a most horrible battle.

Edward stopped. It was no secret that a fleet was being constructed on Lake Erie. The letter gave no other details of size or number, for Kate's mother was discreet.

"I am not alone, my dears, for your Uncle Elias is here with me. He came not long after I sent word of what happened to your ship. There is no reason to think we are in danger here and the house is well hidden by the cedars. Still, the presence of my beloved brother gives me great comfort."

"They would not burn our house, would they, Kate?" Anne asked worriedly.

"I truly hope not." Kate began to laugh. "Is it not rich, Edward? Each of you is helping to build the ships that will be used to fight the battle on Lake Erie. The sailors who crew *Detroit* will slaughter my countrymen, and whoever sails on the vessel my father helps to build will kill as many British as they are able."

"What would you have me do, Kate?" Edward did not hesitate to ask her, but he dreaded the answer.

"Nothing. I cannot ask you to shirk what you see as your duty any more than I could ask the same of my father. But, oh, Edward, it is so very heartbreaking."

C H A P T E R
T E N

The days passed and slowly *Detroit* began to resemble a ship of war. There were other vessels in the British squadron. The *Queen Charlotte*, *Little Belt*, *Lady Prevost*, and the *Chippawa* might all sail out against the American fleet when the day came. *H.M.S. Detroit* was to be the flagship, though; when completed she would be the largest vessel on Lake Erie and Barclay would command her and the fleet.

Edward found Fort Amherstburg to be a strange place. The homes of the men who had been instrumental in founding the settlement were fine large buildings overlooking the river. But many of the public buildings were noisy and shabby. Often they were crowded with bored or anxious soldiers who talked endlessly of the horrors of war. Americans had been slaughtered at River Raisin that January, and in May the fighting had been fierce and bloody at Fort Meigs, just a few days' march away. Tecumseth had been there at Meigs, Edward learned, and he wondered if Paukeesaa had fought by his father's side.

Kate and Anne avoided these public buildings and stayed in and around the camp. Edward went to the Navy Yard each morning. For him the days went quickly. He labored until his muscles screamed with pain, and the sweat poured from him in the hot sunlight. He took pleasure in seeing the ship come into being, and the meticulous work took his thoughts from his uncle. Anne was happy enough. She ignored anyone who did not please her, played with the local cats, and made a fast friend of the fort's goat, which followed her everywhere like a badly smelling dog.

Kate, however, seemed more miserable than ever. Edward had cautioned the girls not to wander about as they had on the island. Barclay had assured their safety, but there were many rough fellows here who might not care to listen. So Kate stayed close to the tents, seldom venturing to the trading post, and only then, in Anne and Edward's company. She grew wan and quiet, but when Edward tried to talk about what worried her, she would only smile and say, "It is just the war, Edward. It preys on my mind."

Released at last from his responsibilities at the farm, Pierre paddled down the river and joined them.

"I thought perhaps it was time I came to the fort," Pierre explained to Edward. "My father decided I could be spared in spite of the fact that I clearly do most of the work. They somehow will manage without me. Besides, I was certain you could not deal with the girls on your own and needed my strength of character to bolster you."

Learning Pierre had some skill with wood, Bell convinced him to work by Edward's side. Together they went to the ship each morning, taking on whatever task Bell had for them. The long oak planks went into place over the frames of the vessel's hull. They used pegs and treenails to fasten down both the internal and outer planking, as well as the deck. Later there was oakum — hemp rope soaked in tar — to pack into the seams to make her watertight. Edward showed Pierre how to fill the seams perfectly. It was messy work and soon their clothing was streaked with black.

"I can spare the shirt — I have another — but Kate made these trousers, and if I ruin them she will have my head," Edward said. "And the heat, Pierre. If it gets any damper and warmer, we might as well be building this ship in the tropics!"

"Then we will not wear trousers at all," announced Pierre.

"Ah! There is a plan! I can barely wait until Barclay sees us. Hardly Royal Navy style, Pierre."

Pierre had no such indecencies planned, though. Long rectangles of wool or even soft cotton would suffice. "My father wears one now and again, and your uncle lives in one summer and winter. The breechcloth is a noble garment, Edward. Light, comfortable, cool. Tie it well now, with the sash around your waist, or the ladies of Amherstburg will faint."

It was a practical piece of clothing, Edward discovered. His shirt hung to mid-thigh and it draped over the breechcloth. He was modestly clothed, cooler, and most comfortable. He paid little heed to Anne, who laughed until she wept. Kate, always sensible, nodded in approval.

One hot afternoon a few weeks later, Kate stood watching them, a covered basket over her arm, her haversack slung over one shoulder. Edward and Pierre both worked stripped to the waist, their shirts tied around their middles, for it was close and humid. The sun shone dully behind thin clouds, but its heat was intense.

"You will burn," called Kate. "You are both tanned, but the sun is fearful. There will be no sleep for either of you tonight."

Edward pulled his shirt over his head. "You are correct," he called back. He was happy for an excuse to cover himself. He scarcely noticed how the young women who came now and again to watch them at work smiled and tittered behind their hands coquettishly. But he was conscious of Kate's assessing look, even if she had only his healthy well-being in mind.

"I will continue to labor in my natural state," Pierre boasted. "We LaButtes would not let the mere sun dictate to us how we dress."

"He is hopeless. I have new cucumbers here," Kate said to Anne. She patted the covered basket. "I will chop and mash them to make a cooling paste. Pierre will need it."

"How does one say boiled crayfish in French?" Anne cheerily asked Pierre.

He turned his amused face to answer her, but there was a crash and a shriek as one of the men fell from the deck of the ship to the ground. Kate ran to him and dropped to her knees. Like most of the laborers, he was from Quebec and had little English, so with some difficulty, she learned that he had no broken bones. He sat there swearing mightily in his patois, rocking back and forth, and holding his head as Edward translated.

"He mashed his ear against the wooden support there," Edward told Kate. The man swore again. "It is painful."

"It will not hurt so very much when the pressure is relieved from the bloody swelling," said Kate soothingly, and, although the man could not understand her words, her tender and concerned tone gave some comfort. "Anne, do you recall where the low water is, just beyond the trees out there? We walked past the spot with Pierre and Edward one evening last week. And I know you have been going there alone, although I have warned you not to do so. Do not deny it!"

"I deny nothing, Kate. You are far too bossy," Anne responded archly. "But, yes. They are prime hunting grounds."

Kate dug around in her haversack and pulled out a small corked jar. Opening it, she sniffed the contents, shook out the herbs, and handed it to Anne. "Off you go then. *Monsieur*, you will come with me," she added in halting French.

"Where are you going?" wondered Pierre. He had come down from the ship and stood nearby Edward.

"To get leeches!" Anne cried with great excitement.

"By the bells of Ste. Anne's, that is disgusting." Pierre looked as though he might vomit. "Tell me you do not pick up such creatures."

"Oh, yes! With joy," Anne laughed. "I will go at once."

"Not alone, you shall not," Edward ordered firmly. He did not have a sense of the countryside being safe anymore. Many hundreds of Natives had arrived in the weeks past, all following Tecumseth, every one eager for the battles that would come with the Americans. They were in the woods and fields; one large camp was across the river from the fort on Bois Blanc Island. Anne was just a slip of a thing and had no more care for herself than did the fort's goat. Edward did not like to think of her wandering alone amongst so many strangers all armed to the teeth. "I will come with you."

"And leave your duty, Mr. MacNeil?" Bell cried.

"I am a volunteer," Edward reminded him with as much deference as he could muster. "I will return when I have made certain that Anne has what Kate needs to tend to your injured worker, Mr. Bell."

Stopping to splash cool water from a bucket onto his face, Edward picked up his musket and set out with Anne. Kate was correct. Anne knew exactly where to go, Edward realized with dismay. She had surely been wandering the fields beyond Amherstburg and the fort, as always, disobedient to Kate and completely fearless. He had been so caught up in the building of the ship that he had forgotten her. He felt a shameful rush of heat up his neck and face that had little to do with the sunburn he knew was beginning.

Anne slipped her hand into his, trusting and friendly, and the guilt worsened. "It is just here," she said. Ahead lay a long pool of shallow, muddy water. Anne was, as usual, barefoot, and she waded in. There were branches and small logs along the edge of the pond. Anne flipped one over, squealed happily, and plucked out two leeches.

She was grinning in triumph and carefully examining the leeches through mud-spattered spectacles. She put the creatures in the jar and showed them to Edward.

Edward would do many things, but he would not have picked up a leech for any reason. "They are excellent leeches. Most impressive," he commented. "But you need not hold it quite so close to my face. Come, let us return so that Kate may do whatever she feels compelled to do with them."

Kate was compelled to apply one to the poor man's ear. It was late in the day. Work would have stopped in an hour or so, but the accident had brought it to an abrupt close with Bell's permission. Back near their tents, a half dozen men watched as Kate bathed the victim's ear and carefully applied a leech to the worst of the swelling.

"My mama, she used to do the same," said a man in his rough English. He nodded in approval. "This girl knows the old ways."

"It gives me the shivers to see it, but it does work," agreed another.

By nightfall, word had spread that Kate was a healing woman of great talent. She could do anything for a person. Moreover, the little sister knew all there was to know of the mysteries of leeches and such. These fine young girls were so far from home, true, but was not every man amongst them in the same boat? And they laughed loudly at the excellent joke.

"All for a leech and bit of salve," Kate said in amazement. She was spreading a cooling mixture of mint and cucumber across Anne's red nose. With a rueful smile she passed the bowl to Pierre. "It will soothe your shoulders and back — yours as well, Edward."

Later they walked along the river. Anne wandered along ahead of them, picking up odds and ends from the beach. Kate walked between Pierre and Edward, all of them talking and laughing. A passing soldier looked the three of them over, sniffed, and passed by.

"If I did not know better, I would say there was some poorly hidden meaning in that fellow's sniffling," Pierre said, looking back over his shoulder.

Kate was silent, looking down at the ground, and although she smiled, her laughter had ended.

"Are they treated well here?" Pierre asked Edward late that night. It was too warm to sleep in the tent, and so they lay on blankets on their backs, looking up at the stars.

"After today, I think that every man who works on *Detroit* will be watching out for them," Edward laughed. Then he became serious. "Anne is oblivious to everything but animals and insects, and Kate will not talk at all. She is wretched, I think. She says only that the war worries her." Edward rolled on his side and faced his friend. "I will take them back to their family myself, Pierre. Are you game?"

"I will follow you anywhere, *mon ami*." Pierre flipped over. "When?"

"They will launch the ship tomorrow if all goes well. Then the masts must be stepped and the rigging done. In a few weeks, as soon as the moment seems right and the weather is fair, we will set out in the sailboat." He stretched out again on his back, his arms behind his head. The night air vibrated with the sound of insects.

"Of course, I will help you in this," Pierre said, and Edward smiled in the darkness, knowing that Pierre could not resist the prospect of a new adventure.

"Excellent. We will take great care to pick the day — there must be no threat or danger to the girls — and we must take great care to keep it secret from the men at the fort."

"And from my father," groaned Pierre. "He will have my skin when he learns what I have done."

"By the time we confess, it will be over. Kate and Anne will be safely back, perhaps this war will end, and I . . ." his voice drifted off.

"What of you, Edward?" Pierre asked bluntly.

"I will not return to England," Edward announced with conviction. "I have not written my parents to tell them of this. I am not even certain a British ship could get letters to England with the American privateers as busy as they say." He paused. "No. That is a lie. I have been putting it off because of the possibility of Uncle John's death." There. He had said it. It was solid and real. If John MacNeil had passed on, then he, Edward, was left here on his own. The words caused him a great aching, almost like a cold knife entering his heart, and yet saying them was a relief. There would be no more pretending. "I will make my home on his island, Pierre, no matter what happens." He smiled a little at his bitter-sweet decision.

Pierre laughed softly. "Your uncle would like that very

much." He sat up, crossed his legs, and leaned on his knees. "Have you spoken to the girls of this?"

"No. Perhaps tomorrow. But there will be so much excitement here, I may just wait."

That night Edward had a dream. Sewn in his hammock, a cannon ball at his feet, men carried his stiff body across the deck of a shattered ship. I am not dead! he tried to scream. Just as the board upon which he lay was tilted, just as he began to slide toward the water to the sound of muskets firing, he awoke in a heavy sweat, his cheek marked with the pattern of the grass on which his face had rested.

He was silent at breakfast, and the unnaturally closed expression he wore kept Kate from asking how he felt.

Anne, though, was not as reserved. "You look odd. Are you excited, Edward? It will be a grand day, will it not? May I stand very close to the ship?"

Edward shook off the weight of the dream and smiled at Anne. "It will be grand, you must not stand too close, and, yes, I do feel satisfaction at this," he admitted, for today *H.M.S. Detroit* would be launched.

All four of them walked to the Navy Yard. Then Kate and Anne stood watching while Edward and Pierre joined the work party. Along each side of the vessel, wooden rails were now constructed. Slowly, carefully, Edward and Pierre worked with the other men to remove the props and scaffolding. The keel was raised with wedges, the ropes that held the ship onto land were cut with axes, and, with a shuddering groan, *Detroit* slid into the water. Heavy hawsers tied to pilings held her moored in the river.

A crowd had gathered to enjoy the occasion. They laughed and cheered and applauded noisily at the launching. Women sat on blankets, babies in their laps or at their breasts, wide straw hats covering their heads. Children ran about insanely or stood silently, awed, with their fingers in their mouths. One small boy had found a stick. He marched up and down, the stick held over his shoulder like a musket. A dozen little fellows followed him in a stiff parody of soldiering. Local men who had no work to do in the fields, mingled with passersby, the hard sort who trapped or traded, or spent much of their time with the Natives. Everyone watched with great interest.

A few of the wealthier landowners sat on their skittish horses, looking down upon the roughly clad locals with the same disdain Edward had seen all his life in England. Canada is very different from home, he thought, but some things are the same everywhere.

Only the Natives were somehow separate from it all. There were many of them; Edward knew the tribal names — Fox, Miami, Odawa, Shawnee. They leaned with casual insolence upon their muskets, watchful and silent. Some were dressed nearly the same as the whites, in trousers and cotton shirts. Others were not: their heads shaved back to a scalp lock, their bronzy skin tattooed, they stood there clad only in breechcloths. There was an unspoken threat in their manner, in a way that seemed to hark back to a time long ago when *they* — not the whites — called this land theirs, and Edward felt his scalp prickle.

Most of the people were speaking French. The whole length of the river had been French at one time and most still was. Then above the chattering and laughter, in a clear, fine tenor, a man began to sing. Edward had not heard the song for a long while. The sound of "Heart of Oak" lifted above the murmuring. Another, then another, voice joined in, and then all the people stopped to listen.

Come cheer up, my lads! 'Tis to glory we steer,
To add something more to this wonderful year;
To honor we call you, not press you like slaves,
For who are so free as the sons of the waves?

None were, Edward knew. There was a freedom on the sea that nothing on land could equal. The song went on, brave, filled with promise, and purely England. Then the last lines rose into the sunlit day.

Heart of oak are our ships, heart of oak are our men;
We always are ready, steady, boys, steady!
We'll fight and we'll conquer again and again.

"I could hear them singing that on the warships when I first went aboard *Marie Roy* in Plymouth harbor," Edward recalled as they walked back to their camp. "They sang it with as much joy then as they sing it now." It had seemed like a grand song, and it was, for it stirred the crowd and anyone who knew it had sung along. How thrilled I was to hear it then, he thought. How I longed then to be standing on the deck of a British ship of war rather than my family's merchant vessel, for where was the glory in that? Now he thought that perhaps he would be quite content with those familiar decks and the crew.

"It is a beautiful ship," Anne said to Pierre. "You must be very proud of the work you did." He smiled and shrugged as if to say it was nothing. "And you as well, Edward. Do you not agree, Kate?"

Edward waited for Kate to say something. He would welcome anything other than her silence.

"For once we agree, Anne," Kate said, smiling gently at Edward. She knew how important the work had been to him. "In spite of all else, she is a beautiful ship."

◇ ◇

Though the women led their children away and the soldiers went back to their duties, the festive air did not disappear. Later, when the evening meals were finished and smoke from cook fires, redolent with the odors of soup and stew, hung in the air, people came back to stand and exclaim over the ship. Someone had a small lap harp. Another carried a fife.

Pierre heard the sound of music just beyond their camp and his eyes brightened. He went into the tent and brought out his precious fiddle. "We have worked hard. Now let us celebrate!"

Edward thought this was an exceptional idea, and Anne loved a gathering for any occasion, but Kate, having just returned from the river with a bucket of water, said nothing at first. She set down the bucket and wiped the back of her hand across her forehead to smooth back loose strands of hair.

"Under the circumstances, I think I cannot celebrate the launching of a British ship of war," she said hesitantly.

"That is not it at all, Kate," Pierre assured her. "We have all had enough of work and when that happens, one must seek release from toil. To sing and dance is an excellent way to do this."

Kate considered this. "I would only go to listen."

Anne screamed with excitement and jumped up and down. Pierre offered her his arm, and the two of them went off.

"You will come, will you not?" asked Edward. He would take little pleasure in the night, he realized, if she were not there with him.

"I shall. Will you wait for me?" asked Kate. She was untying her apron. "If I am to go to a party, then I must be presentable."

She carried the water bucket into the tent. When she emerged a few minutes later, her face was freshly scrubbed and her hair hung loose down her back. Edward thought to offer her his arm. He nearly did, but then Kate began to walk and said, "If we do not go now, Edward, it will all be over."

It was as though the entire camp — the soldiers who could get away, the women at home, and anyone who had been there for any length of time — was letting out a huge, breathy gust of frustration and fear. What better way to do it than with music, dance, and a jug of rum passed round the fire? Pierre played his fiddle and its cheery sound mingled with the harp and the fife. Rather frantic versions of *The Isle of France* and then *The Gallant Poacher*, both somehow measured out so that people could dance to them, sounded quite merry.

And dance they surely did. Sets of couples, all bent upon the pleasure of moving to the happy music, danced jigs and reels for hours.

Edward stood watching. He had had little to do with the soldiers here. They were decent men, it seemed to him. He saw them in the streets and in and around the fort. They were of many ages, from tender boys who did not really need to shave, to older men, clearly experienced in the business of war. From a distance with their red coats, they looked like flocks of cardinals that had settled upon the countryside.

Edward had more in common with the fellows of the Provincial Marine, for they were sailors, and they had often come down to *Detroit* to comment upon her rate of progress. And they had every right to, for it was these men who would sail her.

"Don't be a fool, Ned," one of the sailors called out in response to the bragging of a soldier. "You may have that red coat of yours to tell the world you are at war. We need no such thing, do we lads?" A group of his companions, all dressed liked him in blue gingham shirts with black neckerchiefs at their throats, called out in agreement. "We have *Detroit*!"

The wrangling began in earnest — which regiment was the finest, which would gain the greatest glories in battle — the sort of grand tales and boasting that had always echoed around military fires and meant as much as the cold ashes the next day.

Edward shot a momentary glance at Kate. If she could hear them, she was ignoring the commotion and, in fact, she seemed to be enjoying the music and the excitement. Her cheeks were pink, her head was held high, and she was tapping her foot in time with Pierre's fiddling. Edward looked beyond her.

There was Lieutenant Garland slowly walking toward them. An officer would not be coming out to join this common play. Surely he was only here out of idle curiosity, or simply to take the evening air, for it was horribly hot. The image of Garland gracefully bending over Kate's hand came into Edward's mind and he turned to her.

"Will you dance, Kate?" Edward asked suddenly.

"My feet are bare!" she laughed. "It is too hot for shoes and you will tread on my toes. Besides, I came only to listen."

Edward took her hand and bowed over it. He had done this many times before when meeting young women. It felt a bit odd to be doing it dressed in a breechcloth and with legs uncovered, but such was the convention. He glanced over to where Garland stood watching. The officer smiled, made a small bow, and then walked off into the darkness.

"Very well, I will dance," she agreed. "I cannot resist Pierre's music."

Edward led her out to where other couples stood on the grass. Another fiddler had joined Pierre and the others who played, and the music was beginning again.

Beyond their festivities, Edward could almost feel rather than hear a deep throbbing from Bois Blanc Island. Whether it was the pulsing thrum of night insects and tree frogs or something else, he did not have time to consider, for just then there was a crash. Two men were fighting. One pushed the other into the river, his friends pulled him out, the fighters embraced, and the jug was passed round again.

Edward heard a young fellow, a very young fellow, ask Anne to dance in a voice that wavered a full octave. His face turned as bright a red as his hair when she agreed. She would only begin with this fellow, of course, as Edward would begin with Kate. Dancing here was a social event and it was most rude to dance all night with the person with whom you arrived. Isolated and far from neighbors, people took advantage of such an evening to gossip and share news.

Round the circle they went, hand to hand, person to person. Now and again someone who had had too many nips of the fiery liquid that passed for drink here stumbled just a bit. When the fiddlers gave a great flourish and stopped, the dancers groaned with joy and relief. The women fanned their faces with their hands, laughing and whispering about the handsome partners with whom they had danced. The men clumped together, talk inevitably turning back to the war.

"I will show them to you later, if you care to see," one red-faced man offered. He stood with a group of coarse types, dirty men, unshaven and foul-mouthed. "They are fine and silky, the best I have ever taken, and I know

I can get a generous price for them." He chortled and it was a heartless sound. "You would not ever guess just which gentleman in this town collects them."

"You will not tell us, will you?" taunted someone. "But will you tell us whether they are women's? Those are the finest."

"Women's, men's, and children's! All nicely stretched on hoops." The man leaned forward and whispered something to his companions. There was low, eager laughter and that was when Edward saw Anne standing near them, trying to puzzle it out.

His face darkened. "Come along, Anne!" he called sharply. "Kate, we should return. We have work to do tomorrow and I have had enough of this." He stared at her, his expression insistent and stern. Kate had never seen him look this way.

"A moment, Edward." Anne hung back. The men were beginning to speak loudly again. But Edward pushed her ahead of him. "Kate?" he said, though it was not a question. His eyes flicked to the men. Kate, understanding at last the intent, angry set of his jaw, followed.

"One more set of dances! My fiddle is just warmed to it," shouted Pierre. "I will return shortly." Edward waved and nodded, for the music was already starting and Pierre was focused on his playing.

The walk back to the tents was silent. Once there, Anne bid Edward a good night.

"I did not mean to speak so harshly to you," Edward began awkwardly.

"You were not harsh at all. And I thank you, Edward,"

Kate said softly, just before she followed Anne into the tent. "I could hear what that man said, and I knew of what they were bragging. Anne is not a little girl. She will always seem so to me, for she is my sister, but I would not have her hear of such things."

"Nor would I," Edward whispered. "I am only sorry that you did." It had been scalps of which the men had spoken. Scalping had gone on here for a long while, long before the French and English arrived. The bounties had gradually come about; they were willingly paid by collectors or those bent on vengeance. It sickened Edward to think that Anne might hear of women and children, as well as men, dying for such a reason.

Kate smiled sadly and went into their tent. It took a long while for the music to die down, for the people to stroll away to some place or another. Gradually, the sounds of the evening slowed and faded, and as they did, other sounds became louder.

Very late in the night, Edward lay awake on the grass listening to the echo of drums coming across the river, for that was what that throbbing had been all along. While the people of Amherstburg had reveled on this hot summer night, another celebration was taking place on Bois Blanc Island. Sweat dripped down Edward's back. He lay on his belly, his head pillowed on the shirt he had removed in a vain attempt to cool himself. Kate and Anne were asleep, their tent flaps open for any stray breeze. Pierre had returned after a few hours and was now snoring, half in and half out of the other tent. His hand was on his musket.

They are only drums, Edward told himself. You have heard them before, so put them from your thoughts and sleep. But he could not. Edward sat up, his hair stuck to his head with sweat. He picked up his shirt, rose to his feet, and walked to the river. The sound of the drums was steady.

It was no cooler here. Sometimes a breeze came from out on the lake, all damp with the smell of weed and the pungent scent of the river. There was none tonight. Edward looked back to the camp. All was motionless and quiet, Pierre was a light sleeper and a deadly shot — he was as capable of protecting the girls as Edward was himself, and as devoted. They were in safe hands. A single bat skimmed the river and disappeared. A nightjar called. Edward dropped the shirt in the sand, pulled off his moccasins, and waded into the river.

He had done this many times during these last few weeks at Amherstburg. It was only a few hundred yards away. Pierre would not try it; he was not the strong swimmer that Edward had become. It was all a matter of knowing the current, of judging the angle at which you must make your way out. After that, you just let the river carry you. That is how you swim across to Bois Blanc Island, Edward had explained more than once.

The water crept up past his knees, up to his bare thighs, and past his waist. The current was very strong here; he had retied the waistband of his breechcloth with a double knot to make certain he would still have it when he waded out. There was no musket with which to struggle. He had a rigging knife in a sheath at his waist, and recently he had taken to wearing another small knife that hung around his neck in the manner of the Natives. The wolf pendant was at his throat on its short cord of leather.

Edward dived then, and the water closed over his head. It was deliciously cool, like silk upon the skin. He began to swim with steady strokes, trying to think of nothing but the river and island. He did not know it, but the rhythm of his strokes began to match the beating of the drums that were pulling him to the shore as surely as the current pulled him downstream.

Edward felt the day and the foul conversation he had heard at the dance wash from him. He dived deep and swam with strong, angry strokes.

He popped to the surface for a deep breath of warm air. If he misjudged, he would be carried off and out into the lake to swim back if he could. However, Edward had judged well, and in a few minutes he waded ashore near the south end of the island. His body felt heavy after the lightness of immersion and the muscles of his arms and legs tingled pleasantly. He pulled off his breechcloth, wrung it out, and tied it back around himself, then he twisted his hair to wring out the water. The tie was gone and so he combed it out with his fingers. Then Edward began to walk.

The drums were calling to him, of course. He did not bother to pretend to himself that he had swum across to simply cool off. That such a thing should move his very soul, that the beating and undulating song lifting into the night should make his heart beat as hard as the drums themselves, was madness. But the Oneida blood was there in him; half of what coursed through his veins was just that. He could feel that blood lifting his spirit as the sounds grew louder.

I will only stand here and listen, Edward thought. I have no weapons that would matter. I have swum across the river and stand on the edge of a Native war camp armed with only two knives. Swimming to the island during the day had meant little, but now with the warriors rousing themselves to war, it was a different matter. It was perhaps the most foolish thing he had ever done in his life.

No one noticed him. No one had heard. Many men were in a clearing. In the center, six warriors were seated around a huge drum. They beat it in unison, singing while other men danced. It was a feast, Edward understood. He could smell the roasting meat and his mouth watered. Women carried pots of food and set them before the men, who dipped in with their fingers.

"You are either very brave or very stupid." It was Paukeesaa. Soundlessly, he had come up behind Edward. "Did you think you would not be noticed? They saw you swim from the mainland, and word came to my father that you were on this island the minute you stepped ashore. He says if you do not come within the circle, he will be insulted. That would be most unwise of you, Edward."

Like the other warriors, Paukeesaa was painted for war, the left half of his face coated with vermilion from hairline to jaw. He wore a necklace of bear claws around his neck and silver bracelets around his arms. He led Edward across the clearing and no one paid any note;

clearly, they had been warned that this young man was to be welcomed. As before, Paukeesaa translated.

"You are bold, MacNeil," Tecumseth said solemnly. He was bare to the waist in this heat, smoothly muscled and powerful. "Come sit here and tell me what makes you so fearless. My son has told me many things about you, but not of this courage. Not many whites would have come here tonight. But then you are not white, are you?"

Edward looked for mockery on Tecumseth's face, but he saw only curiosity, as though Edward was some odd sort of creature the other had not ever been able to catch and study before. "I am not white, Tecumseth, but neither am I Oneida. It is a mix of the two. My mother is of the wolf clan." Edward paused, and then added firmly, as though for the first time it had become real to him, "So am I."

"Ah!" Tecumseth gestured toward the pendant. "Strong in battle, a powerful sense of family — you wear it with pride — that is good." He leaned back and stared up at the stars as though he was alone here and not surrounded by men all yearning for battle. "You are wrong, though. You cannot be just a mix, you see. One thing will always outweigh the other. One part must be stronger, or else the two will war within you all your life and you will not find peace."

Tecumseth leaned forward and called out to one of his warriors. The man sprinted across the clearing, fetched something from a woman, and hurried back. Tecumseth took a small pot from the warrior's hands. He gestured that Edward should sit in front of him. Edward hesitated, then sat crossed-legged.

Tecumseth scooped something from the pot — it was vermilion — and smeared it onto the right side of Edward's face. He smoothed the paint evenly across his cheek, along the bridge of his nose, and up his forehead until Edward was painted for war, painted in a mirror image of Paukeesaa.

"Fight with us, MacNeil. Leave the British fort and fight the Long Knives with us. The white blood in your veins is weak and the Oneida is powerful. Do you think it does not show? You cannot resist how it calls to you."

For a heartbeat, Edward almost could not. To cast off the existence he had always known, the civility of England, the order and rank of Amherstburg, and even the adventure of the sea, and to trade it all for this man's world — yes! The drum beat, yes!

He stood slowly, sinuously, in appearance so unlike the Edward MacNeil he had once been that his own father might not have known him. He drew a finger down his cheek and looked at it. It was as red as fresh blood.

"I cannot," Edward said. "There are the others. They are not my family as such, but they are under my care."

Tecumseth slapped his thighs and laughed until his eyes filled with tears that ran down his cheeks. "The girl. The one with the golden hair." He turned to Paukeesaa. "A fine prize, you said? What a wife she would make, you said. Again you missed your chance, my son. Perhaps now another has the prize." Paukeesaa flushed darkly but did not respond. "Go to them then, MacNeil. You will need your Oneida blood for that battle, *Waapi M'wheewa*."

Before he left the clearing with Paukeesaa, he looked

back at Tecumseth one last time. He was still laughing, his white teeth flashing in the firelight. Edward turned away. He would not ever see that smile again.

He and Paukeesaa walked to the beach in silence and then out to the farthest upstream point of the island. In the east, the sun was lightening the sky and the last of the stars had disappeared. A robin sang. Edward waded into the river. He had no idea of what to say to Paukeesaa. How hard it must be to live knowing of your own father's contempt for you, a contempt that was displayed for the entire world to see. No words of friendly encouragement from me would ever make a difference there, thought Edward.

"What did he say in the end?" he asked instead. "You did not tell me."

"*Waapi M'wheewa*? He gave you a name. It means White Wolf."

Edward dived into the water. It felt cold now, like a balm to his soul. He swam hard, as hard as he could, scrubbing at his face, diving repeatedly. When he reached the mainland, the drums had stopped. He picked up his shirt and moccasins. Edward pulled the shirt over his dripping head and forced the moccasins onto his feet. He became aware that already people were about, wandering sleepily to the river for water or preparing to leave in small boats or canoes for somewhere else.

Anne came running. She was in an old nightdress, a shawl half falling from her shoulders. "Edward! You must come! It is Kate! They have hurt her!"

CHAPTER
ELEVEN

Kate stood in the river splashing water on her face, the skirt of her nightdress floating around her ankles. Blood ran from her nostrils; already the neck of her gown was stained a livid red. She was weeping, really weeping, and Edward found that he could scarcely breathe so great was his fury. Very gently he led her back to shore and made her sit in the sand.

"Let me see. I will not hurt you, Kate. There, it is not broken. Who has done this?" he whispered. Then, "Cloths, Anne. Lint. Anything!"

"It was the boys!" Anne shrieked before she ran off. "The soldiers treat us with respect. They have all been so kind, but not those boys from the village. They have been at Kate for days and she would not let me say a word to you. American doxy, they call her. They dared not call me anything, for they knew I would fight back, but Kate would not."

With the clean cloth that Anne brought, Edward gently dabbed at Kate's face while he held her. There was a cut on the bridge of her nose where the stone had hit her. It would leave a bad bruise. She was rubbing one thigh where another stone had struck.

"I was walking to the privy and they set upon me. They are just badly bred little boys who have no one else to torment. I think they did not really mean to do this," Kate said in a tired voice that still hitched. "It has been words only until now, and I should have really fought back, but I did not and so they became bolder. There will be no revenge, Anne," Kate cautioned, for Anne was breathing hard and her eyes were wild. "I will lie down for a while, I think, Edward. My head aches. Anne, there is an ointment of trillium, in a small jar. It is labeled. Bring it to me and it will help stop the bleeding from the cut. A cool compress will end the nosebleed."

Edward was still holding her closely. His heart was thumping very hard; his mouth was dry. He helped her up, but he did not release her. "It is enough, Kate. I will take you home to Sandusky." He stroked back the damp hair from her face. "I wash my hands of it all."

"You are my dearest friend, Edward," she whispered. As she looked at him more closely, her face slowly filled with horror. She touched his cheek and rubbed her fingers together. They were pink with the last traces of vermilion. "What is this, Edward? What has happened?"

What had been so strangely exciting an hour ago, now seemed foreign, even to him. "It is nothing, Kate. Truly."

"Are you certain?" He nodded and she pried herself away. She walked very gingerly to the tent with Anne's arm around her waist. Edward watched them in pained anger, but Pierre watched Edward.

"How long have you loved her?" Pierre asked him.

"I have no idea," Edward answered faintly. Had it started during the long winter on the island when he first became aware of how he valued Kate's companionship? Was it this spring when she had refused to leave him and it had touched his heart so deeply? Or had it been from the very beginning at Fort George, when both of them, shy and clumsy, had first met? "All along, I suppose."

"Have you spoken of it to her?"

Edward's manner changed. His face hardened and his entire body went stiff. "I have not." Then his shoulders drooped. "Look at me. How could I, Pierre? No matter how we say otherwise, no matter how we pass over it each day, we are on opposite sides of this war, and perhaps even in different worlds. We swore it would not come between us, and I think our friendship is strong. It can go no further than friendship, though, if we are to salvage even that."

"I said I will help you and I will." Pierre reached out and gave Edward's shoulder a punch. "You are my friend, eh? Mine as well as hers and Anne's, and we will do this together. There is something to be said for simple friendship, you know."

In the tent, Edward found a towel and a piece of soap. He must scrub away the last of the paint. When he reached the river, he looked toward the wharf where his small sailing vessel was tied. Two sailors were just stepping off the boat. Every line and bit of rope that had once been the standing and running rigging was in their hands. The boat's small blocks had been left behind.

"What are you doing?" Edward called furiously. He ran to them. "Set down that line!"

"I told you there would be trouble," fretted one man. He dropped behind his companion, for Edward, though young, was strong, well muscled, and in a rage.

"Now, MacNeil. Calm yourself. It is the skipper's order, don't you see. All line and blocks are to be used for *Detroit*, us being so short of it and all. We have left you your blocks, though, since they are far too little for *Detroit*."

"Lay it down." Edward's voice was low and steady. All his life he had taken orders and obeyed them willingly. Now he had had enough of it; to give willingly was one thing, but this was thievery. The men stared hard at him, puffing out their chests and grumbling, and then they carelessly tossed down the line. There was something about Edward — his breeding or his stance or the way he held himself — that bespoke a long line of command. He could not see the leader he was or the man he was to become, but they could.

"It's on your head then, when Barclay learns of it," called one of the fellows as they skulked away.

Edward scrubbed his face hard and toweled himself until the skin was nearly raw. He returned to the camp with the coiled lines over his shoulder lest someone else snatch them up. Tossing them to the grass, he went into the tent. When he came out he was in a fresh shirt and trousers, his hair plaited; all suggestion of a young warrior was gone.

He picked up the coils of rope and went toward where

Detroit was tied. She was a hive of desperate activity now. They had begun to raise the masts, a job that might last weeks. There was the bowsprit to set in, and then miles of both standing and running rigging to be put in place.

The commander was not there, but Garland stood by watching the men and speaking to Bell. "Good day to you, Edward," he called. "You arrive for work and with line at that!"

"The line your sailors were in the process of taking from my vessel, sir," Edward said.

A small circle of silence grew around them. The creaking of the block and tackle as the mast was heaved into place, the calls of men, and the slap of wavelets against the ship's hull were there just beyond Edward's awareness. Only Garland's response mattered. "My pardon, Edward," he said. "I had no idea you would not wish to help with the cordage."

"Help, yes. Have it taken from me without so much as a by-your-leave? No, indeed, sir!"

"Very well. May we have the line, Edward? It would be so very useful." There was only a hint of sarcasm in Garland's words, for he, like the sailors, could see how dangerous Edward might be if truly pushed.

Again there was silence. The circle grew as more ears listened, but then Edward simply tossed the rope to Garland. "Use it well, Lieutenant." And he turned on his heel.

"You will not join us in this, Edward?" Garland called out after him. All sarcasm was gone. Catching up to Edward, he spoke quickly in a low voice. "They should have asked. I cannot offer apologies, but by God, they should have asked you. Come with us, Edward. We need more than rope . . ." His voice trailed off for he could see Edward's expression was guarded.

"I fear I cannot," Edward answered. "I have other responsibilities."

"But what of your duty to us — your shipmates? Are you a man to begin a job and leave others to finish it?"

"Is there not one person in life who will not call upon my sense of duty?" Edward sputtered. "Very well, Mr. Garland, you will have my help finishing the work here, for I will see this through." Edward turned abruptly and strode away.

◇ ◇

By the end of August, *Detroit* was ready. Her masts were stepped, her bowsprit stretched out in a long, glorious sweep, and she was as fine a ship as they could make her. She was armed with a strange assortment of cannons and carronades, everything from nine to twenty-four pounder guns. Nothing matched at all, but Barclay had not received the armaments he needed and so he stripped the fort, leaving it all but defenseless. The guns were exercised twice a day; the boom of cannon and the acrid smell of burnt powder soon became commonplace to all.

Her sails were makeshift, being spare canvas from the *Queen Charlotte*, carefully recut by local makers. But they served her well, and her sea trials were a success, or so Edward heard, for he declined to sail.

"The Royal Navy sailors and the Provincial Marine

are all good seamen. Besides," Edward confessed to Pierre, "I fear that if I ever have the chance to set my hands on her wheel and steer her, I will be lost."

One sunny day on the first of September, the Americans sailed up the river. Their fleet had done so before in August, tacking back and forth in front of the fort, taunting the British to come out. Last month it would have been impossible for Barclay to do this, and so he and his men had watched helplessly as Perry and his fleet studied the British ships and the fort. Today it all had a different feel. Edward stood next to Garland, watching Perry command his ships, listening to the orders called out and the snap of the American flag.

"Why do they not sail out?" asked Pierre. "They are here like apples for the picking."

Edward shook his head. "Commander Barclay is no fool, Pierre. It is a southwest wind. They have the advantage — what is called the weather gauge. Their guns look better, and they have more fighting men and likely more experienced sailors."

"You are experienced, Edward," reminded Garland. "We have not enough seamen to do *Detroit* justice. We must make do with the fort's soldiers and some of them cannot even speak English. They do not know how to fight a ship. You have French and so do you, LaButte. At the least, you could translate orders even if you will not take up arms. Or you may assist the carpenter. What is a ship without a carpenter aboard?"

"I remain with my friends, sir," Pierre answered.

"I must decline as well," Edward answered. "You are

persistent, Mr. Garland, sir. May that persistence serve you well and bring you luck." Edward gave a short bow, and then he and Pierre went back to the camp.

"It is the girl, of course," Garland said suddenly. Edward, however, was out of hearing, and so Lieutenant Garland shook his head and said almost to himself, "Take care, Edward MacNeil. That attraction may be the end of you."

◇ ◇

They planned it out carefully during the next days as September began warm and still. Each evening they spoke in low voices as they sat around a dying fire. Anne could scarcely sit still for excitement, and Pierre's enthusiasm joined hers as the sense of adventure began to grow. They would have to use Pierre's canoe, since the boat could not now be sailed. If they were cautious and went slowly from island to island, the voyage should be easy enough. They would take one tent, their weapons and fishing gear, and only the smallest amount of what they needed to stay warm and prepare meals.

"We will live off the lake," Pierre laughed. "I am an expert fisherman, as all LaButtes are. Have I not made certain we have eaten well these last days? Pickerel is the best of fish."

"I believe I have begun to sprout gills and scales, but, yes, you are a good provider, Pierre," teased Kate. The cut on her nose was healing and the bruise had faded from purple to yellow. Each time he looked at it, Edward felt the urgency to get them away from the fort.

Then one night they finally left their camp. They struck one tent, folded it, and carried it and their gear down to the water. "You will sleep under the canoe," Edward said to Kate. "The sky is clear and you and Anne will be warm and dry."

Edward had a compass and a chart that he had saved from his uncle's belongings. He plotted a course by candlelight with Pierre leaning over his shoulder.

"Here are Pelee Island, Middle Island, and South Bass. West and East Sister look fair depending on the wind. Short hops, you understand. We will judge our route by the conditions. We have the time if the weather holds." Edward paused, closed his eyes and took a slow breath. It was rich with burning maple and the smell of the river. But there was something else. He looked up.

It was Garland strolling along the beach. He was dressed in a fine navy uniform with white facings, white knee breeches, and white silk stockings. Aromatic smoke from his clay pipe scented the air with its sweet odor; when he drew in, the bowl glowed red with the burning tobacco. The brass buttons on his coat gleamed in the moonlight.

"Edward. Pierre. It is a lovely evening, is it not?" Garland bowed to Kate and Anne. From where he stood in the shadows, they could not see his face clearly. "And it appears, if I am not mistaken, that tomorrow will be a fine day for a voyage, if a person was so inclined to make one."

"It would be, yes, sir," Edward answered.

"A canoe, a tent, a few provisions, and someone might do nicely."

"Indeed."

Garland held his hands behind his back and looked south toward the dark lake. "All peaceful, as though it is holding its breath."

Edward rolled the chart and put it away. "The lake often gives that impression, Lieutenant. I myself have learned in the hardest way not to take this lake for granted. I thought it would be a mere pond after sailing the Atlantic. Now I know that what may happen on Lake Erie can be as challenging as any ocean."

"Wisely said." Garland bowed again. "A good evening to you all, then. I am off to a late dinner with Commander Barclay and General Procter. Tecumseth will be there, they tell me. Do you know Tecumseth, Edward?"

"We have met."

"Somehow this does not surprise me."

"Lieutenant," said Kate. "Will Tecumseth's son be there, do you know?"

"Why, I think not, miss. Not the son. Only the father. I did hear something about Tecumseth's son having gone off to pray somewhere. That is a wise thing to do before one goes to battle. May you have fair winds, all."

"And you as well, sir," said Edward with deep feeling.

Garland's shoes crunched through the sand and pebbles as he walked away. He stopped and, without turning around, said from the darkness, "Do not go to Put-in-Bay, Edward. I suspect that would be most foolhardy. Go to West Sister instead. The locals say that nothing ever happens anywhere near it."

C H A P T E R
T W E L V E

They left just after dawn. Once out of the river, the paddling went easily since the lake was calm, and only small
patches of cats' paws ruffled the surface. What light
breeze there was came from the southwest and did not
hinder them. By the time the sun was well up in the sky,
Edward and Pierre had tied scarves over their heads. Kate
put a straw hat on Anne and another on herself, but the
sunshine bounced off the water. In a vain effort to cool
themselves, they continually dipped their hands into the
warm water to splash it over their faces and necks.

Anne leaned over the side of the canoe, trailing her
arms in the water. "If you would let me paddle we could
make much better time," she complained to Pierre.

"If I let you paddle we will go in circles," laughed
Pierre. But he carefully shifted positions with her. Anne
sat at the bow, paddling valiantly toward the low rise
floating on the horizon that Edward said was West Sister
Island. By the afternoon, their canoe was a hundred
yards off the beach on the island's southwest side.

"If we are to breathe at all we must be on the wind-

ward side of this place," explained Edward. Here the
water was very clear. Beneath them, the sand was rippled
and dotted with freshwater clams. Edward saw one snap
shut when a tiny fish came too close. They pulled the
canoe up onto the narrow, pebbled beach of the low
island, which was no more than eighty acres in size.
Vine-covered hackberry trees towered above them. A
short distance away, a living elm lay in the water, its
branches keeping it up, its roots partly fastened to the
thin soil.

"That is touch-me-not," Kate announced. She pointed
to plants with their hanging seedpods growing thickly in
shady places.

"And that is poison ivy," said Pierre, gesturing to the
vines that crept up so many of the trees. "I go no further."

Edward gave a wild whoop and jumped aside. A large
snake was crawling past him, gracefully slithering over
the rocks. It slipped into the water and swam out with
smooth undulations of its long body. Disappearing under
the water, it popped up a moment later, a large fish in its
mouth. Another snake slid toward them.

"Anne, I forbid you to pick that up!" Edward shouted.

"They are not poisonous," called Pierre with a shud-
der. He swatted at the fly that was biting his ankle. "They
will nip, but so will any creature if provoked. Even
myself."

"It is only a little snake." Anne had paid no heed to
Edward and was watching, entranced, as the snake coiled
and uncoiled around her wrist. "Thank you, Edward!
This is a grand place."

"Flies, gnats, snakes, and poison ivy. I may hardly be congratulated for choosing our first landfall," Edward replied.

"Nonsense," laughed Kate. "I will gather some touch-me-not. I have never seen so much in one place before. The snakes will leave us alone if we leave them to themselves, and the poison ivy is a matter of common sense. Besides, there are the birds, Edward. Oh, look at the birds!"

None were nesting now, but flocks of cormorants skimmed close to the surface of the lake. Herons waded with their stiff, stalking gait in the shallows, or poised motionless on rocky outcroppings. Egrets ruffled their fine white plumes and the brassy calls of flickers rang out from beyond the trees.

"We are here for the night," Edward sighed in resignation, but the two girls did not seem to mind the discomfort of the little island. Perhaps it was that they were that much closer to home, but they did not appear to notice the insects and the strong smell of bird droppings.

"I will swim, Kate," decided Anne. "It is too hot to stay out of the water. See how clear it is?"

"Your clothing will be soaked, and in this damp heat it will never dry," Kate said, always practical.

"No sane being swims in his clothing unless it is a necessity or he falls from a canoe," Pierre laughed. "Come, Edward. The other side of that windfall tree beckons to me. It has thick branches, should certain females be inclined to peek."

"Both muskets are primed and loaded," Edward told Kate. "I know you say you cannot shoot, but you need only pull the trigger. We will be just beyond the tree there, only seconds away from you."

Edward and Pierre waded out around the tree to the beach on the other side and there peeled off their sweaty shirts and breechcloths. A wind shadow of flat green water stretched out far beyond the shore. Once stripped to the skin and floating on his back in deep water, Edward felt relief. His hair, unbraided, drifted all around his head. He rose up in the water, took a deep breath, and then dived. The coolness slipped along his body. A school of fish sped past in a silver rush. Edward turned on his back and looked up to the water's surface. There was Pierre floating as though he was flying, with the sun spangling the water with each slow movement of his arms and legs.

I could almost stay here forever, thought Edward. There are worse places to end your days. Something nagged at his mind and for a moment, he nearly remembered the dream. His lungs cried to him for air, he gave a hard push against the sandy bottom, and he broke the lake's surface. He whipped his hair around in a long, dark fan.

Wading to shallower water, he called, "Is all well, Kate?"

"We are perfectly fine. Come back when you will."

The sun had disappeared behind the trees when Pierre and Edward returned. Kate was just finishing a single braid in Anne's hair.

"Yours is too short, Pierre, but I will braid your hair, Edward, and you will braid mine. We are tie mates, after all, and it feels so much cooler up off of one's neck."

It was more than a year since she had first said that to him. How many things had happened since then? Edward closed his eyes and gave himself over to the pleasant feeling of her fingers pulling at his hair.

They made no fire; simply thinking of cooking made Anne want to sweat, she said. Instead, they had a small meal of cold meat and bread. The swimming and long day in the sun had tired them all, and so Kate and Anne lay down under the canoe and quickly fell asleep. There was no need for the tent, for the night was clear and warm. A gentle wind had come up from the lake, steady and blessedly fresh, and the mosquitoes blew away.

Edward woke in the night, his bladder full. A round moon was low in the sky; it would not set until around dawn a few hours later. Making certain the girls were asleep under the canoe, he silently padded to the water's edge where he could not be seen. Edward stood there relieving himself, staring up at the sky so brilliantly lit by stars. A streak of silver flashed in the south; it was a small falling star.

"A soul will be going home to God," he said sleepily under his breath, for that is what his Aunt Jane had always told them. Then it was gone and in the morning, he barely remembered it at all.

CHAPTER
THIRTEEN

They did not leave the island until the sun was well up. The day was once again warm with little or no breeze blowing. Clouds of gnats swarmed above the trees, while in the shallows herons stalked quick, elusive fish.

The canoe loaded and riding lower in the water than Edward cared for, they set out. He steered a course around the island to the west and then north a good distance from its shore. Here the water was deep enough so that the canoe would not hit rocks. Anne sat backward, trailing a fishing line baited with a small bit of raw clam.

They were just rounding the edge of the island to head out into open water when Kate looked back and said to Edward, "I have no idea how your uncle could draw things so easily. Any picture I drew would not resemble an island, or a bird, or even a person in the least." She frowned a bit. "Is that music? Edward! Whatever is wrong with you?"

Edward had stopped paddling. His face was ashen. Water dripped from the paddle he held and he was staring at something. Kate turned back around to see what struck him so, and the sound of "Rule Britannia" became clear. The first volley thundered.

"My God, they have started," Edward said quietly.

The British ships were close together. Edward could clearly pick out *Detroit* from her size and her elegant sheer. The American fleet was very near the British, strung out a long way. Every vessel moved slowly, sails lifting and falling in the light wind. Voices called across the water. For long minutes, they sat there watching in horrified fascination.

"We must get away, Edward!" Pierre warned. "Back to West Sister or on to South Bass or anywhere, but we must get away."

"Not back to the island. They may come ashore when it is all over," Edward called to him. "South Bass."

They paddled hard. Every few seconds Edward glanced back at the ships, which were now wreathed in foul white smoke. The roaring of the cannons, the groan and crash as balls hit an American ship, and now the screams of men filled the air. Anne put her hands over her ears and turned her face away.

Something plopped into the water very near the canoe. "Is someone shooting at us?" shrieked Kate. "Surely they see we are civilians!"

"It is stray shot," Edward cried, and he drove his paddle into the water, turning the canoe sharply. "We must get farther out." Even though they were nearly five hundred yards away from the battle there was still the chance they might be hit.

He saw a cannonball coming at that moment, and

would have sworn it floated in on the air. The ball struck the canoe's hull a glancing blow a bit below the water-line, just as it was at a right angle to *Detroit*. Edward could not hear the sound of the birchbark giving way, but he could feel it. Water gushed in through a ragged tear the size of his fist. Kate tried to put her hand over the hole, but it was behind one of the ribs and she could not cover it. Water poured past her fingers.

"Use a piece of cloth. Stuff in a piece of cloth!" Edward cried. He grabbed a blanket and threw it to her. "Bail with the pot, Anne. Bail!"

"Everything except the weapons must go out into the lake," shouted Pierre. "Lean your weight to the side, girls, so that the hole is not so far down into the water." The tent, their bundles of blankets and clothing, plates, and the small frying pan splashed around them.

"It is still coming in. We will sink!" Kate cried.

It was no good, for with all four of them in the canoe it was still too heavily laden. Edward kicked off his moccasins, rose carefully, and said to Pierre. "Balance her, now. I am going in." He dropped out of the canoe and slipped under the lake with barely a ripple. Above him, he could hear Kate's anguished cries. Edward rose to the surface, flung back his hair, and swam to the canoe.

"She floats better now, and if we keep the weight to one side we stand a chance." Pierre had turned himself around so that he would be able to steer the canoe. "You must move forward, Kate, and take up Edward's paddle." There was another splash close by; droplets of water showered over them.

"I will not! Edward, what are you doing? You cannot swim all the way to that island. Come back up at once!" She reached out for him, leaning over the side, and the pressure of the water outside the canoe's walls shot the wadded end of the blanket out. With a horrified squeal, she forced it back in, but this made the hole larger.

Ignoring her entreaties, Edward said, "Lean over. There. It lessens. Make for South Bass, Pierre. Push as hard as you can. Do not go to the bay, but land on this side and hide the canoe. Can you recall where the cave is, Anne?"

"I think so." Her voice was tight with fear. "The dead tree that looks like a man."

"Good. You will find it. No one knows that cave, and you can hide in safety."

In rapid patois Pierre said, "This is suicide, Edward."

"No," answered Edward in kind. "This distance is not so far. I am a strong swimmer and if I stay in the canoe they may both die. Take care of them, Pierre." The other nodded.

"Speak English! You are planning something!" Kate cried out. Then her pale face went nearly colorless. Edward could see the veins pulsing wildly at her throat. "You are not coming with us, are you?" she whispered in horror. "You are going to the ships. You will be killed, Edward! Do not do this, I beg you. You said you would not leave us!"

Edward was taking deep, deep breaths of air into his lungs and slowly expelling them. It calmed him, and it prepared his body for what he would do. "I am the biggest, the heaviest, and the strongest swimmer. I will join you, Kate. I swear so." Impossibly, a musket ball whizzed past. Another nicked the edge of the canoe. They were being blown back to the ships by the light wind. "In God's name, Kate, listen to me. There is no choice here. Anne, lie down. Paddle now, Pierre. I will find you, Kate. I swear this." He reached up his hand to her and their fingers brushed. Then with one last deep breath he slid under.

Edward swam underwater as long as he could and then slowly he came up. He let himself have one last look at the canoe. It was moving away quickly, tilted at an odd angle and riding dangerously low, but it was afloat. He could not be certain, but he thought he saw Kate's face turn to him. He breathed deeply and dived again. Beneath the water, he could feel and hear the blasts of the cannons. Again and again he dived and swam.

At last when he surfaced, he was very close to the smallest American vessel. He kept his head low in the water, turned on his back, took a long breath, and sank down. Staying close to the ships — for the closer he was, the less chance they might see him — he moved through the lines. He was tiring, not just from the exertion, but from fear, for the battle was fierce all around him. Chunks and splinters of wood flew through the air and landed in the water. Men were screaming and shouting, and the cannon fire was continual.

The hull of a ship, perhaps the American flagship, was gliding by very close to him. He met it just as its stern slid past. *Detroit* was on the other side, flames pouring from her cannons. Shattered rigging and line hung over the sides of both ships. Fragments of wood and debris floated between them. Bodies bobbed in the water, then sank. The British would be throwing their dead over the side to clear the decks, and, for all Edward knew, the Americans were as well.

Edward dived yet again. He must come up on *Detroit*'s starboard side, away from the cannon fire. Down, down he went under the hull, beneath the keel, swimming as strongly as he could. She was only sailing at a knot or two in this light air, but it would take all he had to clear her. He saw the huge rudder move as the sailors tried to maneuver the sluggish ship in such light air. His back brushed against her keel, its wood green beneath the waterline.

Edward came out from under her as a man fell into the water directly in front of him. The man's hair was red. It is Anne's young dancing partner, Edward thought wildly. Long, red ropes snaked and swirled around the fellow's head, and when his body turned a slow, lazy revolution, Edward saw he had no face left.

With a choking cry of panic, Edward struggled to the surface. He was on the ship's other side; she was now between him and the battle. The hull rubbing against his back sent him under once more, as *Detroit* ponderously sailed past. Edward rose gasping, turned, caught a dangling line, and, when he was certain it would support his weight, climbed onto the deck. He slipped, for the planks were wet, and he fell with a thump onto his back. He rolled to his belly and managed to get to his feet.

Something gray was squashed into his shirtfront. He was covered in blood and gore that the sand spread on the deck no longer soaked up. The boards ran with it.

"MacNeil!" someone called. It was Garland. "I will not ask how you come to be here, but by my stars I am glad to see you. Commander Barclay is wounded and has been taken below. But see, they are just surrendering!"

The colors had been struck from the American flagship; no flag flew over her now. But a gig was moving across the water, fighting its way through the wreckage and bodies to another American ship, the *Niagara*. Men climbed aboard and in a moment a blue pennant was raised. There would be no surrender yet. *Niagara* was the American flagship now, and Commodore Perry was aboard her.

On *Detroit*, the rigging and sails hung in tatters. Bare feet pounded across the deck, splashing through the blood. The cannons and carronades were very hot from the repeated firing.

There was no slow match, none at all, Edward saw, to light the powder. They were firing the cannons and carronades by shooting pistols into the vents. It was a desperate scene. With deadly precision, the orders to fire were called out. Edward heard, "Prime! Point your gun! Fire!"

Flames and bits of wad shot out from the cannon's mouths as the balls hurtled toward the enemy ships. The cannons recoiled violently with each boom. Heavy ropes, making up the breeching that held cannons in place, twanged their battle song each time they brought up the recoil. Men ran up and down with buckets of water and charges of powder.

Some of them were fighting because it was their lives: they were soldiers and sailors and their business was that of war. Others lived at Amherstburg and so had a stake in this that went beyond duty. I do not wish to do this, but I must, Edward thought with great sadness and shame. There was the deep knowledge in him that if he did not somehow help this day, he would not be able to live with himself. He picked up a cutlass that had dropped from a dying man's hand and began to hack at the rigging and throw it overboard so that the decks might be clear.

"Good lad!" someone called, but Edward took no notice. For hours, it went on. He saw Garland go down with a horrible scream. Sailors carried him below to the surgery.

"Powder," a soldier called to him. "You, there! Powder!" The powder monkey, the man who carried up the charges for this crew, had been shot in half. They tossed the pieces of his body into the lake.

Edward ran down the companionway. Here the sounds of battle were different. Cannonballs were striking *Detroit*'s hull. One crashed through and smashed into a wounded man, who lay bandaged, moaning with pain. His moaning ceased.

The surgeon, Mr. Young, was working frantically on Garland, who mercifully was unconscious and so could not scream. The lancets and scalpels were in disarray. Needles and thread, lint, bandages, bone saws lay on the

table or floor where they had fallen. Jugs of rum and laudanum for anesthetics were nearby. His hands and arms
were red to the elbow.

Edward ran back up on deck with what powder he could
carry. It was a nightmare of sound, the deep booming of
cannon, the pop of pistols, and the crash of rigging as the
ship was hit again and again. The shrieks and sobs of
wounded and dying men, pierced and torn by shrapnel
or splinters of wood, were horrible. There was thick
smoke everywhere and *Detroit* was now surrounded, not
only by her own ships, but also by American vessels. The
American flagship, *Niagara*, was bearing down on them.

At Edward's feet, a pistol, primed and ready, lay in the
blood. Had it fallen from Barclay's or Garland's hand when
they were wounded? Edward picked it up and thrust it
into his waistband.

Lieutenant Inglis, the officer now in command on
Detroit, gave the order to wear ship. They must turn her
around quickly since the overheated larboard guns were
all but useless. They would continue the battle with the
guns on the starboard side. Men strained at the braces in
a desperate attempt to pull around the yards. Damaged
or jammed, they would not move the way they should.
The men were untrained, not seamen at all, but ordinary
soldiers, and their inexperience showed.

Edward turned to follow the others into the rigging as
a cannon exploded. The powder charge was too great.
Men fell to the deck screaming, but Edward could not
hear them, for the blast had been deafening. The sounds
around him muffled and distant, Edward climbed up

what was left of the ratlines. It was as though he was in a sealed glass bottle and all he could hear was the liquid sound of his own racing heart.

Trying to follow the British flagship, the *Queen Charlotte* was turning as well, but she had no speed; the distance and timing had been misjudged. Edward looked across the space that separated *Detroit* and *Niagara*. A sharpshooter clung to the American ship's rigging with his legs. He fired, reloaded his musket, and aimed at Edward. Without thinking, Edward pulled out the pistol, turned his body a bit to make himself a smaller target, and pulled the trigger.

There was no sound. He felt the recoil of the pistol in his slippery hand; he saw the smoke and smelled his own rank sweat. He would never know whether he had killed a man that day, for at the instant he fired, the *Queen Charlotte*'s bowsprit rammed through the wreckage of *Detroit*'s mangled mizzen rigging and Edward lost his grip. Down he went. The pistol splashed into the water. He would have died when he struck the deck, except that he had become tangled in the torn ratlines that swung wildly about. The fall was broken, but his head hit hard and he lost consciousness.

When he woke, it was to the horrible vibration of the American flagship raking *Detroit* with cannon fire. The British flagship could not move, for she was still caught fast to the *Queen Charlotte* in an awful dance of death. Men picked him up.

"I am not dead," moaned Edward as his dream came to life. They were going to throw him overboard.

"We know it," a sailor assured him. Edward could not hear the words, but he saw the sailor smile as his lips moved. "It is just below we are taking you."

Edward looked up. *Detroit*'s ensign was nailed to the mast in defiance. On the *Queen Charlotte*, a white flag of surrender was rising to flutter like a captured bird. A single cannon roared out from the starboard side of *Detroit* to signal her capitulation, and she surrendered as well. It was over.

◇ ◇

Detroit still was afloat, but, like the other vessels, she needed repairs. The British were placed under American guard while work proceeded. Anyone who was not badly injured was given a task. Sails were salvaged and the deck cleared of rubble. Much of the rigging was in shambles so the vessel was jury-rigged with line and whatever canvas they had. Edward's hearing had gradually returned. The bandage they had wrapped around his head was soon soaked with blood, and so, during a pause in the work, he went below to get another.

The surgeon was wiping his hands on his bloody apron. There was a soft moaning as a wounded man gritted his teeth against pain. Two sailors were just pulling a fold of canvas over a dead man's face. They began to sew the dead man into his hammock. He and others would be buried at sea later that day.

"What of Lieutenant Garland, sir?" asked Edward. Garland's body lay on a piece of new canvas on the floor of the surgery. "Will he be buried in the lake as well?"

"Commander Barclay tells me no — I thank God *he* has survived his wounds," Young answered. He pinched the bridge of his nose and rubbed his eyes. "It seems we will sail for Put-in-Bay in the morning. The officers will be put to rest there."

"Who will sew him in his shroud?" Edward asked.

Young turned, wiping a scalpel on his sleeve. "You could be the one to do it. They tell me you knew him."

There was waxed twine and a heavy needle. Gently Edward folded the canvas around Garland. He caught a sickly, sweet odor. The cabin was hot and close and already the dead were beginning to smell. Edward swallowed several times, tucked the canvas around Garland's face, and began to sew. The sailors carried their dead shipmate out and onto the deck. There they would add a cannonball to weigh down the corpse.

Edward worked in silence. On a ship at sea, it was tradition to run the last stitch through the dead man's nose to make certain he truly was dead and not merely unconscious. Edward could not do it. He knotted the last stitch in the canvas, patted the shroud tenderly, and went back on deck.

That evening, one at a time, the bodies of the sailors killed in the battle were slipped over the side while the American chaplain read the service. There were more American sailors than British or Canadian to be put to rest, since so many of the British dead had been thrown over into the lake during battle.

Someone, perhaps a shipmate of one of the dead men, gave a ragged sob. This is how it happens, then, Edward thought. No one will know where they are. No one will be able to sit by their graves or build memorials. How will their families ever make peace with this?

He watched the last canvas-wrapped shape go over, heard the heavy splash of the body hit the water, and saw it sink instantly. Will the iron ball at its feet take it straight to the bottom? Edward wondered dully. Then he caught himself. No, he thought. *His* feet. That was a man.

CHAPTER
FOURTEEN

Late that night Edward lay in a hammock below the ruined deck of *Detroit*. He could hear the pacing of the guards and, now and again, the hollow thump of a musket as its butt was rested against the deck. Somehow, this was worse than the battle. Edward could not sleep. It was not the horror of the battle nor the bloody scenes he kept seeing, even with his eyes shut. Nor was it the wounded men around him who moaned so pitifully. What kept him awake was the thought of Kate and Anne and Pierre. Did they live? Were they securely hidden away? How would he rejoin them now? When dawn came, he was still tossing.

In the morning, the ships — both victors and conquered — returned to Put-in-Bay. The dead officers would be buried there. Slowly, gently, the corpses were lowered into boats. Edward helped carry down the body of Lieutenant Garland, while the bands of both squadrons played solemnly. Guns on *Detroit* and the *Lawrence* fired, and the sound brought the battle sharply to the front of Edward's mind.

On the shore, a procession formed by order of rank, alternating the American then the British dead, with the shrouded bodies of the most senior officers coming at the end. The surviving officers somberly followed, walking two by two, American, and then British.

Edward watched as men lowered Lieutenant Garland into the earth. The chaplains read the rites, a songbird called off in the woods, and Edward stood there with tears streaming down his face. He did not weep for Garland or anyone else. He would never speak of it, but the tears he shed were not tears of grief. Edward wept because in that instant he was so very grateful to be alive.

Many hours before, a sailing vessel, the *Swift*, had ghosted through heavy dawn mist into the cove at Pêche Island. She was an old boat of some fifty feet with graceful lines. Two half-pound brass swivel guns were mounted on her rails. The man who sailed her was tired to the core of his very soul. He had come a long way — in his anguish, he sometimes thought that he had sailed to Hell and back again during these bleak months — but now despair had at last changed to resignation, acceptance of his nephew's death. Lord John MacNeil had come home.

John knew Pêche Island was the only place he might restore himself. When Julian and Pierre LaButte had brought the news of Edward's drowning, his mind had nearly snapped. The entreaties of Julian and his son were as meaningless as if they had been speaking a foreign language. He had to get away, far away, for he could not face the thought that he had lost yet another MacNeil placed under his protection. Tucked into an isolated island cove in Georgian Bay, his grief was as cold in his heart as the harsh winter, whole days and weeks of time were missing from his memory. He had not wept once.

But spring and then summer had come, and one soft morning as loons cried to each other in the distance, John had sat on the deck of the *Swift* and sobbed. The next day he slowly set sail for home. He would bring word of their son's death himself to Jamie and Sarah. No letter could ever tell them how sorry he was.

He dropped the anchor. In the light air, the boat swung slowly around when the anchor bit into the sand. The canoe he towed behind his vessel made a soft thump as it struck the hull. Without thought, he folded the sail on the boom and tied it securely, folded the jib, and tucked it away in the small cuddy that passed for a cabin. He picked up his musket, since he would no more venture anywhere without it than he would his document case.

John stopped. The document case had been left behind in his home when he set out. He thought then that he might never feel the desire to draw again, that he would never more take any pleasure from life. Perhaps in time that, too, would pass. It had done so before.

He went ashore in the canoe and pulled it high onto the sand. The small sailboat was gone. Thieves had likely been at work. In what state would he find his home? He started toward the house and then he paused, drawn inevitably to the orchard. Knowing he could not fight the impulse, he changed direction and set out for the trees.

John MacNeil carried his six and sixty years well. Time had etched lines onto his face, but his striking gray eyes had not changed. His long hair, clubbed in an old-fashioned manner, was silvery. Something about him bespoke a man who had lived in another age and, in some ways, still did. He wore leggings and breechcloth and a shirt of rough, worn cloth that had once been very fine. His manner was confident and calm.

Sunlight would burn off the mist, but for now it was dense and grew thicker as John went into the forest. It was very still, very quiet. Water dripped from leaves with tiny plops. He smelled wood smoke and heard the low singing at the same time. He did not believe in ghosts — though he might have. Still, the hair on the back of his neck lifted and prickled.

Slowly, soundlessly, John stepped into the orchard. Mist swirled around the figure that kneeled there facing the unseen sun that rose beyond the trees. It was a young Native. He was singing, and John realized with a wrench that it was a death song that he had not heard since he was a boy long ago.

> *When it comes your time to die,*
> *be not like those whose hearts are filled with fear of death,*
> *so that when their time comes*
> *they weep and pray for a little more time*
> *to live their lives over again in a different way.*
> *Sing your death song and die like a hero going home.*

"Who are you?" asked John. His voice, unused for so long, shook and croaked harshly, but the musket he held pointed at the Native was quite steady. The young man staggered as he rose to his feet. John could see that he was painted for war. Streaks of red and black colored his face and upper body. "Who are you, I say? What business have you here?"

The Native's musket was out of reach. His eyes flicked to it, but he would be dead before he could touch the weapon. "I am Paukeesaa, son of Tecumseth. I have come here to pray since this is a sacred place. Where better to prepare for death?"

"Death?"

Paukeesaa lifted his chin. "The war. Men die in war. If my father dies, I will die with him." Paukeesaa gazed hard at the man. "Will you tell me who you are?"

"I am Lord John MacNeil. What has happened here?"

Paukeesaa laughed. "You are Edward's uncle, then! He talks of you often. You have been away and may not know that the Long Knives are at war with the British, and it has reached us here."

John lowered the musket; in truth, he nearly dropped it, he was so bewildered. "My nephew. He is alive?"

"As alive as I am. He stayed here for a time waiting for you."

John ran to the house with Paukeesaa following. He threw open the door and looked frantically around the room. Then he saw the letter on the table. With trembling hands, he unfolded the heavy paper and read Edward's words with the most profound joy.

*If you are reading this, my dear Uncle John, then you
are alive and must know that I am as well. No one has
taken your belongings. I have them with me at Fort
Amherstburg. Make all haste to join me there, Uncle,
for I long to see you.*

John looked up, tears in his eyes, and he laughed shakily.
"Edward is at Amherstburg." He started as the words sank
into his mind. "By all that is holy, if it is war here again,
I would not have him there. I must go to him at once."

"It is possible that Edward may still be there at
Amherstburg, but there were two girls under his protection."

"I know this," John said impatiently. "Edward was
escorting them to their parents."

"He spoke of crossing the lake to take Kate and Anne
home."

Paukeesaa's time for prayer was finished and so he would
accompany Lord MacNeil back to where Tecumseth
waited with his warriors at Fort Amherstburg. They left
John's canoe on the beach and set out in the *Swift*, tow-
ing Paukeesaa's canoe behind them.

As they sailed down the river, Paukeesaa told the older
man all that he knew of Edward and the young women.
Then their talk shifted to the war.

By the time they reached Fort Amherstburg, John's
anger was enormous. "Always war. Always the military or
the Navy or the Crown," he murmured ardently to himself. "Will the day come when we are beyond the reach
of all this?" For now, only Edward mattered.

There was little or no wind, which had frustrated John greatly, but it made sliding up against the wharf a small matter. There was a crowd on the shore. Soldiers there caught the lines and made them fast. John and Paukeesaa leaped off.

"Lord MacNeil! My stars, sir, it is amazing to see you," called a young fellow. "Have you come to speak with General Procter?"

"I have not," snapped John. "My nephew Edward — is he still here? That is my vessel." He gestured to the small sailboat tied nearby. "Most of it at any rate. I see scavengers have been at it. Where is he?"

"They say he went out into the lake two days ago," someone called out in Shawnee.

"Is this so? You know Edward MacNeil, Paukeesaa. Are you privy to his plans?" It was Tecumseth. The crowd parted; soldiers and Natives and curious civilians made way for him. He regarded his son's face carefully. "You are painted for war, once more, Paukeesaa."

"I am. I will fight by your side, Father."

"There will be no need for that — not here at least." Tecumseth laughed hugely. "It is almost certain that the British ships have taken those of the Long Knives, you see. The war on this lake is won. We will have our lands back and the old ways will be with us once more."

"Where did they fight?" John asked urgently in Shawnee. "When?"

Tecumseth tilted his head to one side in surprise, for not many whites spoke his tongue. It was poor Shawnee, but he could understand him. "The smoke from the guns made it hard to tell, but it would have been near West Sister Island. They have not returned, but that means nothing. Warriors feast and celebrate after a victory — Barclay had a bear on his ship that he planned to slaughter for the feast. We, too, shall celebrate when our lands are returned to us." He cast a cool look at John and then asked Paukeesaa, "Who is this white man with whom my son keeps company?"

"I am Lord MacNeil, Tecumseth."

"Ah, yes, the uncle of Edward. Your ship could have been there to help win the victory and bring us our rewards that much more quickly. You missed a great chance, but perhaps your nephew did not. He is a warrior at heart, you know."

John was thinking only of Edward and the girls' safety. He cared nothing for this Native, yet he could not help himself. He stood very close to Tecumseth and said in a quiet voice, "I have lived here longer than you. I have seen what they have done to this place, how long ago they purposely spread smallpox to kill the Natives, how women and helpless children were slaughtered all up and down the frontier in their wars. You have seen it as well.

"War is one thing. It is around us like the very air, but when we breathe it into our souls, then we are lost. You are a warrior. You lead your people to their fate." Then in English he whispered, "Do you think for one moment that the British will keep their promises to you when every promise they have ever made to your people has been broken?"

Tecumseth drew himself up to flip back a sharp answer,

but something in Lord MacNeil's eyes stopped him. Tecumseth loathed the whites and what they had brought about. He always would, but this man was different. Clearly he was *okima* — a leader — much like Tecumseth himself. "I have no choice," he whispered back in the same tongue.

MacNeil nodded slowly. He needed to say nothing more on the matter. "*Pesalo*. Take care, Tecumseth. I go to my nephew." He crossed the wharf, boarded his boat, and began to cast off the lines.

Tecumseth turned from Paukeesaa. The moment had passed and his mind was already on other things far more important than a son whom he considered to be not only a coward, but far too white in appearance.

Paukeesaa thought to call out, to follow his father but then he did not. He owed Edward and the females nothing now. They had seen him at his weakest, but the memory of the gentle, pale hands of the girl Kate and the laughing eyes of the younger one, Anne, strangely moved him. He ran down the wharf and with a great bound landed on the deck of the boat as it was moving away.

John did not ask for an explanation. Paukeesaa offered none, and so they sailed down the river, out onto the lake, and across to West Sister. John cursed the light air, but slowly the wind began to pick up from the west. That evening they anchored off the island and went ashore to call for Edward, but there was no answer.

"Where would they have gone?" asked John in frustration. There was no despair in his voice now, only a fierce determination. Then he turned to Paukeesaa, his eyes narrowed. "You know, do you not?"

"I do. They will be under the earth," Paukeesaa said with assurance. "The place is *ta'hapiya siikwi*, the sacred cave where I stay alone, the place of crystals."

CHAPTER
FIFTEEN

It was a wild, rough sail to South Bass Island. The wind had begun to blow steadily while they searched West Sister, and now the wavelets that had at first skittered past became waves and then small rollers. The *Swift* was an elderly vessel, but she had always been lovingly and painstakingly restored each spring. In spite of what John now asked of her, she would answer. Both sails were filled as *Swift* sped across the lake away from the setting sun. By the time they came round the east side of South Bass, the sky was a deep indigo and the last of the sunset's brilliant colors were fading.

John would not normally have anchored in so exposed a spot. The lake was unpredictable and the wind was growing stronger. A boat could drag and be lost. But there was a bit of shelter here, and *Swift* was riding the waves easily enough with two anchors set into the sand. Besides, nothing mattered if his nephew was lost to him again. All that John could think of was finding Edward and the others.

They hauled the canoe up to the long grass, away

from the grasping waves that rolled along the beach, and set out. They carried blanket rolls over their shoulders. "If they have been in the cave for any length of time, they will be cold," Paukeesaa said.

Darkness was an ally now. They ran through the woods and brush, unseen, unhindered, while the wind rushed through the trees above them. Once John felt the patter of raindrops. He looked up to see a raft of clouds sailing past the moon. Paukeesaa silently gestured for him to stop. They waited, listening, staring into the darkness where the trees opened and the woods ended. There was no sound but the wind, no smell of wood smoke, no laughter or talk.

"It is empty," John said with certainty. "Not a person is out there."

Still, they went carefully. Paukeesaa guided John to a spot near the center of the field. Just beyond it was a huge old tree whose nearly bare trunk shone like white bone in the moonlight. He dropped to his knees, pulled back the grass, and called down into what John could see was a hole in the ground.

In seconds, Pierre's head popped up. He began to say something to Paukeesaa, but then he saw who stood nearby. "John!" he cried joyfully. "We never gave up hope that you were alive! *Mon Dieu*, Edward will be so happy to see you!" Pierre heaved himself out and reached down for the hand that Anne extended to him. He pulled her up.

"Is Edward below? Bring him out, for the love of God." John's voice was insistent and harsh.

"He is not," answered Pierre. He could barely look at Edward's uncle, concentrating instead on helping Kate out. Both the girls were shaking from the cold, dank air of the cave. Their skirts, still damp from the flooded canoe, flapped heavily about their legs.

"What has happened?" John asked with growing fear.

Kate wrapped one of the blankets around Anne, whose teeth could be heard chattering. She flipped the other over her shoulders and said, "He thought only of us, sir. He swam to the ship because our canoe had been hit and it would sink otherwise. He is on *Detroit*." Her chin trembled and she looked away. "He is the bravest person I know, Lord MacNeil," Kate went on in misery. "I am so fearful that he is a prisoner."

"He will not be a prisoner for long, miss, if he is," said John in grim determination.

They walked hurriedly back to the beach, with the wind roaring through the oaks above them, talking along the way, explaining to Paukeesaa and John all that had happened. They had not made South Bass Island at first in the leaking canoe. They could see that soldiers were on the shore watching the battle, and, fearing they might be captured, they had paddled for nearby Rattlesnake Island. In the morning, they had crossed over to South Bass Island and hidden in the cave.

"We would not have done so, but Edward said he would return to us," explained Anne. "He would never have found us anywhere else."

"Before we left Rattlesnake, we watched the ships go by as they sailed to the bay, but could not tell whether the British or the Americans had won the battle," explained Pierre, shivering violently. "We could see Edward on *Detroit*. He was at her wheel.

They reached the edge of the beach where Paukeesaa's canoe had been left. John and Paukeesaa picked it up and carried it to the water. The wind was fierce now; their clothing blew flat against them, and their hair whipped across their faces. *Swift* was there offshore, pulling hard at her anchors.

"Could you see pennants or any flags as the ships sailed past?" asked John. He held Anne's hand in a firm grip. "Into the canoe with you and hold tightly, child. The waves are large."

"Only the American flag and a blue pennant with some white letters sewn upon it. I could not make out the words," Kate shouted back as the canoe shot out into the lake. "I could see no flags on the British ships." She gasped when chilling spray hit her face and ran down her neck.

No one spoke again as they made their way back to the *Swift*. John and Pierre went aboard first. Pierre helped up the girls while Paukeesaa tied the canoe to the *Swift*'s stern and John prepared to set sail.

When the anchors were raised and the mainsail and jib up, John pulled hard on the tiller to turn *Swift* and run her downwind. Wiping sweat from his face with the back of his arm, he said, "The Americans have captured the British squadron. There is no doubt of it, and so Edward is a prisoner of war. I swear they will not have him. No matter what I must do, I will not leave him in their hands. They will not have one more drop of MacNeil blood while I live."

John steered while Pierre did his best to trim the sails. It was hard work, for the wind was up and a gale was surely coming. Kate had settled Anne in the small low cabin; Anne shuddered with the cold and wiped furiously at her spectacles with the hem of her skirt. Kate pulled off her own blanket, covered her sister with it as well as she could, and said to Paukeesaa, "I will help Lord MacNeil." She called out to John, "I can sail, Lord MacNeil. Edward taught me. Paukeesaa, please hold Anne."

Paukeesaa drew back. "Hold her?" he cried incredulously. "Why should I do this?"

"Because she is just a young girl and half-frozen, and she actually does seem to enjoy your company, although I cannot imagine why!" screamed Kate. Then in a lower voice she begged, "They need my help. For pity sake, hold her until she grows warmer."

"There is Madeira in the cuddy," John called out. He braced himself hard as the boat rose and then rode down a steep wave. There was a steady thrum in the rigging; *Swift* vibrated with the force of it. "Get a swallow of that into her, man. There are tin cups as well."

"My sister does not drink spirits, Lord MacNeil," Kate said primly as she moved to the stern of the boat. "And neither do I." She took the mainsheet from Pierre and he trimmed the jib.

"This is very good," Anne shouted out. Paukeesaa passed the bottle across to Pierre and wrapped his arms around Anne. She smiled up warmly into his face. Pierre took a draft, John swallowed a mouthful, and then he passed the bottle to Kate. The tiller in his hand, he gave her a long, stern look. Kate knew that look, for she had seen it on Edward's face when he had pulled Anne away from the scalper during the dance. Kate had no strength left to argue. Taking the Madeira from him, she sipped a small mouthful, swallowed, and breathed deeply as the heat hit her belly.

Even with the boat running downwind, John could feel of the strength of the blow that was approaching. Then *Swift* came briskly around the northeast point of South Bass and headed into the bay almost directly into a twenty-five knot blast. But once in the lee of the island with its tall trees, the water abruptly flattened. Quickly Pierre and Kate dropped and bundled the jib; they would sail in on main alone. The boat heeled sharply even with reduced sail, skimming across the protected water. They took her across in a series of easy tacks. Many ships were at anchor within its shelter, all pointing into the wind. A few voices called out as the *Swift* passed silently through the fleet, but no one made a move to stop her.

"That is *Detroit*," Pierre said in horror. "At least what is left of her."

Even by moonlight, they could see that the ship was nearly destroyed. It seemed a miracle that she still floated. Her hull was pocked with many holes, her bowsprit was gone, and what remained of her rigging was a pitiful shambles. A reek of smoke still clung to her, and the brown streaks that ran down her sides could only be dried blood. How much blood must have been shed that day? John's hands shook to think that his nephew had gone through the hell of such a battle.

A few sailors of the Provincial Marine and several armed men who were clearly American guards watched cautiously as *Swift* neared. Pierre hailed a man who stood on her deck.

"Is that you, young LaButte and, my word, is that Lord MacNeil?" came the incredulous answer. Other voices called out to Kate and Anne.

Kate dropped the sail and they tossed lines up to the men on deck. "Is this a good idea, sir?" one sailor said uneasily to John. "We are captured and all prisoners of war. They may take your boat and you as well."

"Edward MacNeil. Is he on this ship?" asked John, ignoring the man's warning.

"He is, sir. Below with the officers."

Not waiting for anyone else, John picked up his musket and climbed onto the deck of the ship. An American sailor moved forward to challenge him, then thought better of it, for not only was this man fiercely intent to go below, but the British seamen on deck were all bristling in support of the stranger. The prisoners outnumbered the guards. Instead, he wisely ran ahead calling out that someone was coming.

With no ceremony at all, John entered the small, lamp-lit cabin, peering about for Edward. He had not seen his nephew for a very long while, not since he had left the boy aboard the *Marie Roy*. He was not prepared for the sight of the young man, tanned and self-assured, who stood there in profile. He held a hammer in one hand. Clearly, he had been nailing on pieces of boards to patch holes in the side of the ship.

Two tired officers — one British and one American — who were sitting at a table in earnest but tense conversation stared at the intruder. Edward was just turning around. At first there was no expression on his tired features, but then as he realized who was crossing the room, his eyes widened, his face blanched with the shock, and his knees nearly buckled. He walked slowly forward and wordlessly embraced his uncle.

John could not speak. He swallowed hard several times. "Oh my dear, dear nephew," he whispered. "We have both come back from the dead, Edward."

One of the officers coughed slightly. It was the American. He was a young man, serious and somehow still grimly precise in his blue uniform coat in spite of the day's dreadful work. "Our problem is solved it seems," he said.

"Commander Barclay, Commodore Perry, sirs, this is my uncle, Lord John MacNeil." Edward made the introduction as well as he could, but the polite formality after the carnage of yesterday nearly choked him.

"We had just spoken of you, sir," said Barclay wearily. He, too, wore his dress uniform, gold epaulets at the shoulders. His arm and leg wounded, he had lost blood and although he was alive, he was clearly worn out and low in his spirits. "How fortunate you arrived. Edward would have gone along with the ships. Not as a prisoner of war, mind you, but there was nothing else to do with him." Barclay turned his gaze to Perry. "I trust this suits, sir? He is not actually attached to the ship or to the Navy at all, as I explained."

"It does, I suppose, sir," Perry answered, though he did not seem completely convinced. "I will say that it is highly irregular. I suppose young MacNeil could not help the fact that his canoe was so damaged by your cannon fire. Nor could he do much at all about being pressed into service." He shot a fleeting look at Edward and said dryly, "There has been precedence after all."

Pierre and Paukeesaa were with *Swift*, fending her off from the side of the ship, but Anne and Kate had hesitantly followed Lord MacNeil onboard. Now they waited in the passageway outside the cabin where they were sheltered from the wind. Unable to restrain herself any longer, Kate peeked around the doorway. There was Edward, covered in blood. Crying out, she ran into the cabin.

"What have they done to you, Edward? Oh, no, you are hurt!" She touched his head, then his cheeks, and ran her hands down his arms, her eyes flying over him.

"Most of it is not mine," Edward answered soothingly. "I am not much injured, but my word, Kate, it is good to see you." He held her away from himself and looked her up and down, his heart hammering. She was shaken and white-lipped, but she was alive. "Anne and the others?"

"Pierre and Paukeesaa are outside, but I am here!" shrieked Anne. She sprinted across the cabin and threw herself into Edward's arms. "Oh, Edward, I was so afraid for you!"

"All is well," he murmured. His arms around Anne, he faced Kate with great urgency. "We must leave at once,

Kate," he went on hurriedly. "I will tell you everything on the way back to the island. When this war is ended, we will sail you home to your parents as soon as you wish. You have gone through more than you ever should have, Kate, but all of that is finished now."

She put her fingers over Edward's lips to stop the flood of words. "It is over," she said simply. "There are American ships here, Edward."

"What of it? No one on them will harm you or Anne. I am released from here and we have safe passage. Tomorrow we will be back at Pêche again and all will be just as it was."

Kate shut her eyes with the pain of hearing his ramblings and pressed her fingers to her temples. "Listen to me, Edward. They are *American* ships. They will sail home to America." Kate turned to Perry. "Sir, might my sister and I take passage with you? Could you somehow get us home to Sandusky? Until that time I have some skill as a healer and I may be of use to your surgeon."

"Your servant, miss." Perry bowed. "Mr. MacNeil has explained who you both are, Miss Kimmerling. I do know of your father — he is a very fine shipwright. Yes. It will be my pleasure to see that you and your sister are returned home. We will go across to *Niagara* shortly, once Commander Barclay and I have concluded our discussion." Edward began to protest. "Fear not, Mr. MacNeil. These young women will be treated with the utmost deference and discretion. They shall be in no jeopardy, and no one need ever know they are aboard if they wish to remain below."

Edward began to say, no Kate, not this way. Not yet! Before he could utter a word, a sailor came racing down the companionway shouting that the very devil was breaking loose in the bay! The *Queen Charlotte* was dragging her anchor in the storm! "Leave quickly, Lord MacNeil," said Barclay wryly. "Scarcely anyone will notice that you were here in this uproar."

John nodded to the officers and then followed Edward and the Kimmerling girls out on deck. "It is a good time to make our escape," he said. "Into the *Swift*, Edward."

"A moment please, uncle," Edward answered. He turned his attention to Kate. "In time there will surely be peace." Then, uncomfortably aware that he had an audience, he took Kate's hand and led her to the bow of the ship. The lantern that hung there lit their faces, but with the wind, no one could hear what they were saying.

Edward held both of Kate's hands in his and spoke to her. He began to go down on one knee at her feet, but she would not let him, so he said what he had to standing there before her. Then he stopped and waited. She spoke and nodded, and although the wind wailing through the rigging masked the sound of her voice, she had clearly said yes to his question.

Edward lifted first one of her hands and then the other to his lips. With a look of hopeless exasperation, Kate put her arms around his neck and kissed him full on the mouth. Their hair steamed out in the wind, strands of his tangling with hers.

"That was very romantic," said Anne with great interest. "Do you not think that was very romantic, Lord MacNeil?"

"Indeed," laughed John. "Come, Edward!" he shouted. "We must be away before *Swift* grinds herself to bits against this ship."

"I am sorry we will not have time to become acquainted, Lord MacNeil," said Anne, watching Edward reluctantly lead her sister back, Kate's arm looped through his.

"Oh, I suspect we shall be acquainted in time, Miss Anne. Until then, farewell to you and to you as well, Miss Kate." He gave a deep bow and Anne curtseyed with as much style as she could manage. Kate gave him a wide smile.

"Kate," Edward said, just before he went down into the *Swift*. He pulled off his pendant, the wolf that marked him for what he was, and dropped it over her head. "If you need my help," he said very close to her ear, "when you wish me to come for any reason, send this to me, and no matter what, I promise that I shall." Then he climbed into the boat.

Once in the *Swift*, Edward looked up and held Kate's eyes with his as long as he could, while the boat moved away from *Detroit*. With the squadron's attention on the *Queen Charlotte* whose crew was resetting her anchor, few paid much heed to the sloop that cut loose from the ruined flagship, raised its sails, and came about smartly. On *Swift*, Edward's eyes remained fixed on *Detroit* and the two figures that stood on deck, lit by the moon's glow. Neither John nor Pierre spoke to him or urged him to help. He would not have heard them anyway.

Edward watched Kate and Anne wave and wave, then

Anne went below and only Kate stood there, slim and motionless, one hand raised in farewell. He stared until he could no longer make her out. Edward sighed deeply and turned around. "Let us go home, Uncle John," he said in a small voice. "Let us go home now."

It was a bracing sail to the river. The wind was on *Swift*'s larboard side blowing right across her deck. She rode easily, sliding down the waves with a lively motion and a great whoosh of water under her hull. They stood short watches, fitfully dozing on deck. The sun rose up behind them to turn the sails a tender pink and gild the foam on the waves. Late that day they stopped at Amherstburg only long enough to reclaim the small sailboat and set Paukeesaa ashore.

"Once more you have my gratitude, Paukeesaa," Edward said. "When this is done, come to Pêche. And if there is anything I might ever do for you in return, you need only ask. *Pesalo*, Paukeesaa. Take care."

"What is the word? Have you any word of the squadron?" called a soldier. "They say it has been captured!"

"*Pesalo*, Edward," said Paukeesaa, ignoring the man. "May you find peace on the island. One cannot help so there, but my time for peace has not yet come, I think."

He turned and pushed his way roughly through the men; Edward knew that he would be seeking his father, who must surely be there. The last Edward saw of the young Shawnee, he was disappearing into the crowd.

CHAPTER
SIXTEEN

In spite of the fact that they were sailing upriver, it was a speedy voyage. They took Pierre back to his family's farm in Sandwich. Captain LaButte was overjoyed to see both his old friend, John MacNeil, and Edward, as well as his delinquent son. If he felt anger that Pierre had accompanied Edward, he said nothing of it that night. He pulled them inside the house where Pierre's brothers embraced him and cried out for the full story. Pierre's mother and sisters fed them to bursting with what simple food they had. Although Edward longed for the island, and he could see his uncle felt the same way, he put aside the longing and joined in the celebration.

"It will be bad," LaButte told them later. They sat in his kitchen, an open bottle of red wine in front of them. "We were fairly certain the squadron had been defeated. The Americans will come across at any time. I know Procter. He cannot make a stand at the fort — almost every cannon was taken from it to arm the ships. He will burn Amherstburg rather than simply surrender it. It will be a time for defending our homes, John."

⟡ ⟡

In the morning, Edward and his uncle returned to Pêche Island, which seemed to float serenely there in the Detroit River, as though war was not about to erupt around it. Edward had reclaimed the chest containing his uncle's papers from Julian LaButte. They moored the vessels and Edward waded ashore for the canoe so that they might bring in the chest. On the beach, he looked back at *Swift*, and then looked all around himself. The trees were changing color; red and orange leaves were plastered on the wet sand, ring-billed gulls laughed above him in the cloudless sky, and purple asters bloomed in the sunshine. Nothing seems to change here, Edward thought gratefully.

There was work to do, many cartridges to prepare, muskets to clean and reload. They removed the small swivel guns from *Swift* for safekeeping and carried them and the chest to the house. Exhausted in mind and body, they did nothing further.

"You need sleep more than anything else, now, Edward. Sleep well," said John warmly.

Edward wearily prepared to go up. "What of you, Uncle?" He paused at the foot of the staircase.

"I will be up in a short while." John smiled a little. "It is very good to be home once again."

Edward climbed the stairs to the second floor. It was quiet and unnaturally tidy there. No laughter rang in the hallway; no one had left a basket of sewing out to complete. No birds' nests or wilting flowers or collections of shells sat on the small table. Where books had been stacked to be savored while tucked cozily in bed, there was only bare, polished wood. All signs of the girls were gone from the bedroom in which he stood, and yet Edward could still feel them somehow, and he wondered in that strange way that people sometimes do when too much has happened, if it had all been a dream.

But the bloodied clothing he stripped from his body was very real. With a force that was almost painful, the images of the battle swept over him. He stretched out on the coverlet, certain he could not ever sleep again. He caught just the faintest scent of lavender. He thought of Kate. Holding that sweet memory in his mind, he closed his eyes and drifted off.

◇ ◇

When Edward woke, he was not at first certain of the time or day or even of where he was. Then he smelled strong coffee and the odor of frying bacon and he knew he was home. He sat up stiffly and walked to his uncle's chamber. He found clean garments, a bit of soap and a towel, and padded barefoot down to the first floor.

"You look more nearly human than you did last night," observed John critically. "There is food here if you have an appetite."

Edward groaned. "A swim first to wash the last of this foulness away."

At the cove, he waded out into the water. He sank to his knees, scrubbed himself with sand and then soap. He floated on his back for a long while, eyes closed, his ears underwater. The terns crying above him in the deep blue sky were only a faint sound. It made him think of the battle, and so he stood and shook himself, his raw, scrubbed skin prickling with goose bumps.

Later, they slowly returned the paintings and papers to their places in his uncle's library. With a small hammer and short, flat-headed nails, John carefully reattached the paintings to their mounts and fitted them in the frames. Edward and he worked in close, companionable silence, the sort where words are not needed.

There was only one painting left in time. Edward unrolled the portrait of Mack, Owela, and Thomas and handed it across to his uncle. A low fire burned in the hearth, for the day had become cool. There was only the hiss and pop of apple wood, like the song of fall coming.

"She was very brave," Edward said softly. "They all were." When John looked up in surprise, Edward handed him the journal, the locket, and the wampum belt. He went on uncertainly, "I know what happened, Uncle. I read it all."

John was silent for a long while. He fastened the painting to its mounting, placed it in the frame, and hung it. Carefully he slung the locket from its corner. He set the journal on the mantel and draped the belt across it. With a deep sigh he walked to the window and stared out into the night.

"Their memory is so very precious to me," he said almost to himself. He twisted round and round the silver ring he wore on his smallest finger. "It took me a very long time to make peace with what happened to them.

I did, though. Sarah was alive because of Mack, and if I could not take joy in that fact, I would not have honored the sacrifice.

"Jamie married Sarah and in time you were born. What a gift that was to us all. By then I knew that the living were more important than those who have passed on. I loved them and love them still, but they are gone. You are not, I thank God!"

He turned and his face was almost angry. "Why, Edward? Why did you place yourself in such danger? You might have stayed with the canoe. It near killed me to see you on that ship, to think that I might have lost yet one more person I love to any war."

Edward gestured toward the picture. "And take the chance that the girls might die? Or live with cowardice? There are many sorts of bravery, Uncle. Mack made her choice. She could not have lived with herself had she not gone back out into the storm. I made my choice to send the girls and Pierre out of danger and then stand with those brave men on *Detroit*. They fought that day for far more than winning a mere battle. I would not have been able to stare at my own face in a mirror ever again, had I not.

"Now I will stand and fight here if I have to, and defend this island, for it is my home, as it is yours." He gently touched the older man's arm. "You need not shelter me, Uncle John. I am no longer an inexperienced boy. I have seen war's face." He made a sound that was more a sob than laughter. "I want to be standing by your side if war comes here."

John shut his eyes with the pain those words caused

him. He himself had said something very like them to his father on the eve of war a lifetime ago. He only prayed that in years to come Edward's son might not ever speak them to him. Would peace never come to this country?

"My father once said to me that Canada had claimed me for its own. Has that happened to you, Edward? Are you willing to pay the price?" He searched his dear nephew's face, the face so like his brother Jamie's and yet so like that of Edward's uncle, Owela.

"I am."

They began to ready the island for the siege that could come. Water was no problem. Neither was ball and powder, since John had a large cache of it secreted away in small, sealed barrels beneath the cold room. The *Swift* itself would be defenseless, but they had to choose between her and the house.

They rerigged the small boat and then carefully hid it in the rushes, ready to launch. Every gun was primed and loaded, and hundreds of cartridges prepared. The homely tasks of cutting wood, salting and drying meat, and setting aside whatever vegetables they could from the poorly tended garden, kept them busy. There were few deer to hunt; the woods on the mainland had been hunted nearly empty by the hundreds of Natives who had camped in the area. But ducks and geese still migrated as they always did, and so Edward and his uncle took those.

"The river and lake are full of fish," said John. "We will not starve."

"They may not come," Edward said in satisfaction. They had worked hard for more than a week. "If we are lucky they will pass this island by, but, if not, we are ready."

One day they stood on the beach in a cold rain, muskets in hand, and watched scores of war canoes, heavily laden, journey up the river past the island toward Lake St. Clair. It was not only warriors who paddled, but also women, children, and old people. Not a sound came from the Natives in the canoes. A tiny child lifted his hand in greeting. Edward waved back and the canoes passed by.

"They are retreating," said John in amazement. He squinted hard and then lifted his musket in the air. "It is Pierre."

Pierre paddled near the beach but did not come ashore. "I must return to the farm," he called to them. "Others are leaving their homes, but we will stay and fight."

"As will we," Edward called back. "Take care!" He waved as Pierre turned the canoe and headed back across the river, and his friend's brave smile and straight back nearly broke Edward's heart.

In two days, they saw the smoke in the distance, far down the river on the south side where the fort and Amherstburg lay. Or where they once lay, thought Edward. What will we see when we pass there again and when will the Americans come here?

More than a week later, they were still waiting, watching for something to happen, but it did not. There was no gunfire from across the shore, and no sound of cannon or battle from Fort Detroit or Sandwich.

One night Edward walked on the beach, his musket

cradled in his arms, a cartridge box swinging at his hip. It was very cool and clammy, but the drizzle that had fallen all day had stopped. Above him, through wispy cloud, a full moon shed silver light that rippled on the hushed cove.

Edward no longer prayed as he had when he was a child for some favor to be granted or some special object to be his. Now, as he looked up into the sky, he did not even pray for himself. Let her be safe, Edward begged. Let them both be far from here, home and safe.

He decided to go back to the house. Suddenly, there was a splash, a great clatter of wings, and muffled quacking as a duck launched itself into the night. Two canoes had disturbed it from where it slept with its head beneath its wing. His heart drumming, Edward slowly raised his musket and aimed.

"Do not fire." It was Pierre, his father, and someone else. Edward lowered his weapon, looked harder, and saw that it was Paukeesaa. There was something so strange and solemn about the manner in which they landed their craft that Edward said nothing at all. He only waited. Then he saw the long, canvas-wrapped shape that lay there inside Paukeesaa's canoe. Edward watched as they pulled the canoes ashore.

Paukeesaa came very close to Edward. His war paint was smeared and streaked. His deerskin clothing was grimy with mud and filth; the stink of sweat, despair, and something else clung to him. It was the smell of death, Edward realized.

"You said if there was ever anything you could do to

repay me, all I need do was ask." Paukeesaa stared down at the shrouded corpse in the canoe. "Help me, Edward."

◇ ◇

More than three thousand American soldiers had defeated the British and their Native allies at a place on the Thames River called Moraviantown. Many British were now prisoners, and the victorious Americans had returned to Detroit. The fields had been littered with bodies, but Paukeesaa could not leave his father there.

No one saw Tecumseth fall. Some claimed to have done so, but no one knew exactly when it had happened or who fired the shot. Already the Long Knives argued for the glory of it. They did not honor a courageous, fallen warrior. No songs were sung in his memory. There was no feasting. No stories were told. Instead, they had defiled him. It was left to Paukeesaa to do what he could.

Edward walked to the house; he and John returned with two spades. There was no hurry. Together, by the light of a single lamp, they carried the body to the orchard and gently set it down. Then John, Pierre, and Captain LaButte walked back to the house, leaving Edward and Paukeesaa standing there looking down at Tecumseth's still form.

Edward returned alone some hours later. Pierre and his father were asleep, and only John sat waiting by the fire in the front room. Paukeesaa would spend the night in the orchard, for he must pray.

Edward slumped into a chair. "It is done. He said I must dig the grave, for he was forbidden to do so." He held up his blistered hands. "It must face the east. There should have been a stone from the river to mark his resting place, but that would tell the world where Tecumseth lies. I put back the sod as neatly as I could, Uncle. You cannot tell where he is. It will be a small matter to fill in the spot and make it level when it sinks. I promised Paukeesaa this." Edward rubbed his hands over his face, worn to his very essence. "It is to be a secret, Uncle. No one is to ever know the resting place of Tecumseth, and no one shall."

John said nothing. He only listened with complete sympathy.

Nearly numb with it all, Edward stood and went to the staircase. Without turning around he said, "They scalped him and cut strips of skin from his thighs, Uncle. The American soldiers wanted keepsakes. It seems that skin makes very fine razor strops if the tanning is done well." He started to go up and then he stopped. "Paukeesaa is no coward." Then, as slowly as an old man, he went up the stairs.

In the morning, Paukeesaa was gone, and only the dew, as wet and cold as tears, was left to mark the spot where his father was buried.

The war was like some sort of cruel animal feeding upon whatever peace seemed to be left. They fought at Chrysler's Farm near Cornwall. Towns were burned and families lost everything. How many men had died trying to protect those precious things? Would the fighting resume here? Edward knew he would fight just as hard if war turned on them here like the mindless creature it was.

News came in December when a passing trapper brought a packet. It was addressed to both John and Edward MacNeil. Edward sat very still, the packet in his hands. Then he slowly tore it open and pulled out a letter. It was from Elias Stack.

My dear friends. I have taken it upon myself to write to you with the deepest thanks for what you have done for Kate and Anne. They are now safely home, as is their father. I will remain here at Sandusky until I am entirely certain there is no threat to them. I fear it is only a matter of time before the fighting moves to Fort George and Fort Niagara. If so, it is possible that my home will not be there when I return. It matters not. It is only a building and family means all to me, as it does to you.

I regret, Edward, that it is my sister and brother-in-law's wish that Kate and Anne refrain from writing until the war has resolved itself. I myself do not entirely agree with this, but the decision is not mine to make. My nieces' reactions were much the same as mine, but being dutiful daughters, and understanding that their parents' decision has nothing to do with their very high opinion of you, they agreed to respect those wishes — after each penning one last letter, of course. Not even the hardest heart could have refused them. You will find their brief notes enclosed.

My nieces can be very insistent, Edward, and quite dogged when they set their minds upon something they want. I advise you to take heed of this, particularly with regard to Kate.

I give you the greatest joy in your reunion, John and Edward. I look forward to the day when we are once more together around a fire. I dare say you will have more than one interesting tale to tell me. But then, you do know how much I enjoy a good tale.

I remain your most humble servant, Elias Stack.

Anne's note was brief:

I miss you, Edward, but it is most wonderful to have my dog, Kerry, again. Take care with leeches. They can stick with a vengeance. Salt is best. Your servant, Anne.

He read Kate's letter once, twice, and then another time, simply taking intense pleasure in holding a piece of paper that had once been in her hands.

My dearest Edward, I meant every word I said to you that night on the ship. When peace comes, and it must, I will send word somehow. Until then, I remain yours. Love, Kate.

He had no idea how long he sat there alone in thought, recalling all the things he had tried so hard to shelve away.

Behind him, John cleared his throat and asked hesitantly, "Might I ask, is it good news?"

"It is, Uncle. In its own way it is very good news. I will

need the patience of some Byzantine saint to wait it out, but it is good news and I am hopeful. The war cannot last forever."

It would be two and a half years before peace became reality, and for Edward it was longer than a lifetime.

CHAPTER
SEVENTEEN

Very late on a warm night in August, in the year 1815, Edward lay on his back on the cove's beach. John and Pierre were stretched out on either side of him. Beneath Edward, the sand was still warm from the afternoon's brilliant sunshine. He gave a low groan of pleasure, for he had worked hard all day.

Fall would soon sweep over the island in a great cleansing rush. A carpet of yellow and orange would hide the graves, one marked with a dragonfly and one hidden in the orchard. Each winter they had been blanketed with deep snow. And each spring, tender moss and patches of tiny violets came to life upon them once more. Birds nested, apple blossoms popped open, and the entire cycle began yet again.

For all this time Edward had tended the orchard the way his uncle had always done, and the way Pierre's great grandfather had done before that. The task fell to him gradually in the manner that a treasured legacy passes from one to another. He found a deep satisfaction in scything away the weeds, cutting dead branches, and watching the apples grow. It was a good place to work and when work was done, a good place to sit, and think, and savor the peace of it all.

War had not returned to the river or the west end of Lake Erie, although caution was to be observed when traveling the area. A treaty was signed in Europe December 24, 1814, which ended the war there. By March of 1815, the military here received official word of this, and with the scratching of a pen on paper, the war ended in Canada. All the battles — a heartbreaking list of bloody fighting and destruction — they were all gone like smoke on a windy day. Unless you had been part of it.

"In just that way they end it," Edward marveled. "Men fought here even after the treaty had been signed at Ghent. They fought and died even while England was at peace!" Once Edward would have wondered what it would be like to fight. Now he knew, for the memories of the Battle of Lake Erie would never leave him for the rest of his days. He only thanked God for his life and gave thanks for the bravery of the men who had fallen.

Edward and his uncle again roamed the lake and river, for at last John's desire to draw and paint had returned. Sometimes they took the small sailboat or even *Swift*; other days they used the canoe. They never went far, since both of them called Pêche, with its bare beaches and quiet canals, home. The pleasures of those small simple things, a warm house, food in the belly, the close friendship of one's companions, were very sweet.

During the last two years, letters had arrived from England in answer to those sent by John and Edward.

Everyone at Brierly was well and sent their fondest love. And just this month past, word had arrived from Jamie and Sarah that they planned at last to return to Canada. It was obvious that they had to if they were to see both their son and brother. John had been thoroughly Canadian for countless years. Perhaps Edward was now as well.

How wonderful life will be when we are together once again, Edward thought, stretching luxuriously. It will be almost perfect. Almost. He closed his eyes and thought of the one thing that would close the circle of his happiness. With a deep, slow pain in his very bones, he put that thought aside.

"Do not sleep," said his friend, Pierre, driving an elbow into Edward's side. "You will miss it if you do." They were young men now, but Pierre and, in truth, Edward still now and again reveled in nonsense.

"Thank mercy for the breeze," John said from Edward's other side. "There are still enough mosquitoes here to carry off a person. The wind will keep them away and we can enjoy this."

It began slowly. One streaked across the sky, and then another, dozens of tiny falling stars, until there was a shower of light that spangled across the blackness through the constellation Perseus. They were the meteors that fell at this same time every summer. The fiery tears of St. Lawrence, some called them. Kate would have known that, Edward said to himself.

As he lay there, enjoying the starlit sky, Edward heard his uncle unexpectedly sit up and reach for his musket.

Even in these peaceful, sleepy times, they were never without arms. Edward and Pierre sat up as well, and with their weapons in their hands, they all stood. A large canoe was gliding into the cove. Edward could hear the dip of paddles. Someone spoke in a Native tongue. It was Shawnee, Edward realized, and the summer of 1813 came back in a great flash.

The canoe floated just off the beach. Someone stepped out and waded ashore. Pierre and Lord MacNeil watched Edward lower his musket and walk to meet that someone.

"Paukeesaa," Edward said warmly. "I did not think to see you again."

"Nor I you," Paukeesaa answered. Even by starlight, Edward could see that the young Shawnee had changed. His eyes were hollow. His face was severe; a raw scar ran down one cheek.

"Have you come to visit the orchard?" Edward's voice was barely a whisper.

Paukeesaa shook his head. He leaned on his musket and his bleak disillusionment could not have been more evident. "No. That is past. It is all done and past." He straightened and for a moment under this bright sky, he was the brave young warrior Edward had once known. "I came only for this. She said to tell you it is time and she awaits you." He held out his hand, took Edward's, and pressed something into it. Then he waded back to the canoe. He turned before he climbed in and asked, "Did you ever learn what you are, Edward?"

"I did," Edward answered, and there was more than a

little pride in his voice. "I am a Wolf and a MacNeil, and that is enough."

"I rejoice for you. I will not return here. I go upon a journey to meet my fate, and if I am not mistaken, *Waapi M'wheewa*, you do as well." They heard his laughter as the canoe slipped into the darkness. Edward would sometimes think of that laughter and the echo of sadness he had heard as it faded away.

He opened his hand. It was the pendant, the wolf.

"Might I have the use of *Swift*, Uncle John?" he asked. "I have a journey to make, it seems."

⬦ ⬦

They left a day later before dawn. The falling stars that had held them so rapt not long ago sparkled unnoticed above. The *Swift*'s water casks were full and she was lightly provisioned; Edward and Pierre would fish or perhaps hunt along the way. Their stomachs hardly mattered now. All that called to them was adventure.

"You will give my best wishes to Kate and Anne and my regards to their parents," said John. "I look forward to the time we meet. And if Elias is still with them, tell him that he must come to the island. I would wager we have more than one story to share."

"I shall, Uncle." Edward smiled at him and asked, "Are you certain you will not come with us?"

"Perhaps we shall sail on to the east end of the lake, eh? There is a ship there we must gaze upon. They say the *Tecumseth* is a glorious vessel, indeed," added Pierre.

"In time," laughed John. "This is a young man's journey and courting is best done without unneeded advice. I suspect you shall have enough of that from Pierre. Sail well, Edward. I shall be here when you return."

John embraced his nephew, clasped Pierre's hand, and watched them paddle out to the boat in a routine so familiar and graceful it gave him joy. The canoe secure, they cast off from the mooring and raised the sails. Edward pulled on the tiller until the canvas filled. He waved and smiled, and looked very happy. Not until the softly glowing mist swallowed them up did John turn away.

"The orchard will be a fine place to watch the sun rise," he said aloud. It promised to be a glorious day. Perhaps he would spend the morning there sketching before he turned to any work. It would be tranquil and deeply sweet with memory, for if any ghosts had once haunted its shadows, they were now at rest.

Above him, unseen, one last falling star, a huge thing, streaked across the sky, rivaling the rising sun. For a glorious heartbeat, it shone there and then it was gone. John MacNeil settled his document case upon his shoulder and set off, his heart finally at peace.

AUTHOR'S
NOTES

Writing historical fiction can sometimes be a little like tiptoeing across a battlefield. One must not rewrite the facts, no matter how strong the urge. It becomes a bit simpler when the facts are well known and when the history itself is rich and exciting. Then there is only a good story to be told.

Edward MacNeil and his family are, of course, fictional characters. Many of the other people mentioned are not. There are Commander Barclay, Lieutenant John Gardner, and Commodore Oliver Hazard Perry, whose blue pennant with the words "Don't Give Up The Ship" was carried from the *Lawrence* to the *Niagara*. Mr. Bell, Lieutenant Inglis, General Hull, and General Proctor were all part of the conflict on Lake Erie. Captain Julian LaButte and his son Pierre were there as well. They are my ancestors. I have taken liberties with the LaButte section of the family tree for the purposes of this story.

I live on a sailboat in the summer and over the years have had the opportunity to visit many of the places where *Under a Shooting Star* is set. They are as intriguing and moving as I hope I have portrayed them to be.

The cave mentioned in this work is called the Crystal Cave. It is located on South Bass Island on the property of the Heineman Winery; it was discovered in 1888 when they were digging a well. It is open to the public in the summer.

No one knew of the cave's existence in 1812. They did know about the earthquake, however. The New Madrid Earthquakes struck the central Mississippi Valley in the winter of 1811–1812; the most powerful had a magnitude estimate of greater than 8.0. It is easy to imagine its effects reaching South Bass Island.

The fighting and the Battle of Lake Erie were far bloodier and more horrible than I portrayed them. The records tell a very grim story of bravery on both sides. A monument stands at Queenston in Ontario to commemorate General Brock. On South Bass Island in Ohio, The Perry's Victory and International Peace Memorial was built between 1912 and 1915. At the 1913 dedication of the memorial, the remains of the three British and three American officers killed during the battle were reinterred beneath the floor of the monument. Lieutenant John Gardner rests there to this day.

It would be incorrect to talk about war in North America during the 18th and early 19th centuries without including Natives. Every army had its Native Allies. For the British during the War of 1812, Tecumseth and his warriors were as important as this book portrays them to be. The date of Tecumseth's birth is uncertain —

1768 is likely. They say that when he was born a great comet shot across the sky. His name is sometimes translated as "Panther Going Across the Sky". It is also translated as "Shooting Star". Tecumseth's stormy relationship with his son Paukeesaa is well documented.

The graves and the apple orchard on Pêche Island do not exist. No one knows the location of Tecumseth's resting site although there are stories and even a memorial. The truth is a closely guarded secret.

The War of 1812 has sometimes been referred to as Canada's forgotten war. I believe that nothing is further from the truth. It is remembered by all the reenactors who portray the living history of that time whether they are militia, civilians or soldiers. And if *Under a Shooting Star* does anything to honor the memories of the Natives, Canadians, British, and Americans who were there, it will have served its purpose well.

ACKNOWLEDGEMENTS

I am a solitary writer. The quiet of my studio in winter and the deck of my own boat, *Windseeker* I suited me best as I worked on this book. But as always, there is a small army — or perhaps navy this time — of people to thank, people whose advice and support were invaluable.

Both Kathryn Cole and Lynne Missen edited the work, gave me fresh insights and kept me firmly on track. Jennifer MacKinnon worked extremely hard as always to make certain all changes were correctly in place. Al Van Mil once again created a wonderful cover image. My appreciation to all.

Two gentlemen kindly read the manuscript for historical accuracy. My thanks to Larry Lozon for details regarding many aspects of the War of 1812 and the military. My thanks as well to Bob Garcia for the fine points about Fort Malden and the surrounding area.

My appreciation goes to Peter Rindlisbacher for information regarding the Royal Navy, its ships, and other things nautical; to Maria Freed and many other kind people on both the Native and Shawnee lists for help with the Shawnee language and Native culture in general; to my shipmates, the crew of *H.M.S. Tecumseth*, whose brains I endlessly picked; and to all the kind individuals on the 1812 discussion list for patiently answering what must have seemed to be at the time, very odd questions.

Ellis Delahoy, a fellow reenactor, once again placed his persona, Elias Stack in my hands. He has my appreciation for allowing me to decide the course of Elias's life. I thank Karl and Kathy Kimmerling and their daughters Kelly and Kristin, around whom the Kimmerling family in this story was created.

And finally, in some ways my greatest thanks go to my husband Bill whose support has been and remains unfailing.